THE MADDY SAGA

BOOK SIX

I0525746

PONYGIRL SEASON

BY

PAUL BLADES

Cover Art by Agnes Knox
agnes.knox@gmail.com

Dark Visions Publications
darkvisionspub@gmail.com

All characters and events portrayed in this work are
fictitious

Previously published:

Watch for publication of the other books in the Maddy Saga:

Other books by Paul Blades:

Klitzman's Isle
Klitzman's Empire
Klitzman's Paradise
Klitzman's Pawn Part One
Klitzman's Pawn Part Two
The Taking of Cheryl Part One
The Taking of Cheryl Part Two: Slaver's Bait
Comfort Girl No. 4
Sacrifice to the Emerald God
The Blue Cantina: Anna's Surrender
The Warlord's Concubine, Book One and Two
Dreams and Desires

CHAPTER ONE
A DAY AT THE GROBGY ESTATE

Anton Drabik, the cruel, scar faced, former Red Army colonel, sat on his high set stool in the middle of the training ring and watched the unhappy, new, naked, bound and hooded ponygirl make her belabored circuit around it. He held the long, thin dressage whip in his hand and idly tapped it against his right thigh as she made her thirtieth circle around the small ring, snorting and crying, her tall, black boots kicking up the dust, her large breasts swaying and jumping on her chest. The ponygirl was past the need for encouragement until, of course, her pretty, pale white legs and thighs began to tire. Then he would add a few new stripes to her already red thatched rear haunches and get more from her than she believed it was possible to give.

She was a tall, strong, young, Austrian pony, having arrived at the Grobgy estate just today. Axmail Grobgy, a gangster by trade, was a former sergeant in the KGB who had made all the right moves following the breakup of the Evil Empire. He was an infamous runner of contraband of all descriptions and was one of the brightest stars in the criminal oligarchy which ran the former Soviet Republic of Kalikastan, a small nation nestled strategically in the crux formed by the borders of the new Russian nation and the Ukraine. Grobgy was Drabik's erstwhile boss, although Drabik, a former Red Army colonel, often grated at the thought that he was a henchman of a mere former sergeant, even if he was formerly with the security services. But Drabik had his plans and, if all went well, soon the gangster would join his former ideological confreres in Workers' Party Heaven.

The tall and muscular ponygirl trainer had joined the criminal elements of the former proletarian paradise when his regiment was demobilized shortly after the end of the Afghanistan fiasco. He had darkened many a door since then, serving as Grobgy's most feared executioner. Ponygirl training was his hobby; death was his avocation.

Drabik noted that the blond tailed ponygirl had started to falter in her rounds. Of course, the mechanical arm of the training machine set a cruel, mandatory pace for the poor, former human female. It circled the training track relentlessly, dragging the ponygirl behind it over the dry, hard packed dirt. A chain led from the strong wooden arm to the leather shield that covered the pony's mouth and chin. Behind the shield was a thick leather plug which filled her oral cavity and turned her piteous moans and whines into muted protests. She wore a blue Neoprene hood over her head with two little dime sized openings for her eyes which obscured all of her facial features. A hard plastic, leather covered collar was around her neck, higher in front than in back, forcing her head to tilt upwards. A broad leather strap hung from the back of the collar and the pony's writhing, braceleted wrists were confined there. Ponygirls had no use for arms or hands. Over the next few months the muscles in her well toned but now vestigial upper limbs would atrophy into practical uselessness.

The killer issued a sharp blow from the pony whip and its contact with the pony's rear was marked by a loud 'crack!' The frightened pony squealed in pain and picked up her pace. She had tight, firm thighs and broad hips. Her breasts were large, even for her expansive, but gracious torso. Ideal for a ponygirl. She might not qualify for any of the swifter teams, the single pony sulky or the two pony cart, but she was more than suitable for the larger teams, the six pony cabriolet or the nine pony landau. The Grobgy teams were all set for the fall racing season, but you never knew when a pony might pull a muscle or tear a ligament.

Drabik could see that the pony was tiring. Her tall, laced, black ponygirl boots, with which she had been adorned for the first time two hours ago, were beginning to drag in the dirt. Two more laps around the small track and he would give her a rest.

'Crack!' The whip came down viciously on her ass. 'Crack! Crack! Crack!' With each fiery kiss, the pony screeched and lifted her tired thighs higher. Her large, pale breasts danced on her chest wildly. Sweat poured off of her porcelain frame in rivulets. Her long, pale yellow ponytail bobbed to and fro from where it emerged from the tight, head encompassing, blue hood. Dust kicked up where her heavy, black boots landed.

One lap was done. "Crack!' 'Crack! 'Crack!' Drabik gave the agonized pony additional encouragement. She had no way of knowing that this would be her last lap before a short rest period. Her mind would be filled with desperate pleas to her deity, a sense of the unreality of her situation, a wave of self pity at her undeserved, cruel fate.

When the pony passed the lap marker, Drabik shut down the machine that drove the ruthless armature. He yelled the Russian word for 'stop!', "*Vaats!*" It would not take long for the pony to learn the fifty or so words she would need to know in Russian. 'On your knees!', 'Open your mouth!', 'Faster!' No one talked to ponygirls and they obviously never engaged in conversation themselves, being constantly gagged or bitted when their mouths were not in actual use servicing a master's cock or lapping up their high protein, gruelish meals.

The tall, blond tailed pony, not yet understanding the command, took a couple of extra, by now, plodding, steps and the chain that connected her gag to the armature yanked her head backwards. Drabik struck her twice more across her rump, yelling, "*Vaats! Vaats!*" The former human female screeched in pain and ceased her motion. She stood there, her chest heaving, her breasts shaking with each desperate inhalation. It took time to get used to running while breathing only through your nose. But she would get used to it. All of them did.

Drabik let the shapely, naked, hooded female recover her breath. When her snorting gasps for air turned to sobs of misery, he stepped forward and took stock of his new trainee. Her white skin was slick with sweat and her chest was bright red from her exertions. He reached forward and took her heavy breasts in his hands, assessing their heft, teasing the thick, short nipples. She flinched when she felt his hands on her globes, and he pinched the nipples hard to correct her squeamishness. She would have to get used to having her prizes manhandled as well as every other part of her. The sexual use of ponygirls was frequent and callous. A properly trained ponygirl was wholly subservient to her sexuality. The need for physical passion would become imbedded in her personality while all human traits would be driven out.

When the freshly dehumanized creature had arrived at the estate that morning, she had undergone a ritual first use by her new owner, the swarthy, heavyset, black haired Grobgy. She arrived naked, gagged and hooded after a night of transport in a pony van. At the slave reception center where she had been received encased in a long, aluminum shipping tube, her head and pussy had been shaved and she had been attired in her first ponygirl harness and a heavy, leather hood which she still wore when she had reached the estate of her new owner. Grobgy had pushed her onto her back onto a bale of hay, forcibly spread her legs widely and teased her hairless slit into lubrication. A dozen men stood around and called out ribald encouragement as Grobgy penetrated her with his long, thick, steel hard cock and slowly, deliberately, brought her to pleasure. At the moment when her enforced passions began to overflow, the tape which had been used to cover up her eyelets in the hood was whipped off and she was able to see the grinning, appreciative face of her assailant and owner. She undoubtedly recoiled at the cruel visage, the long, black, heavy moustache, his piercing, cold, blue eyes. And she sobbed and moaned her misery as her pussy's convulsions proved her whorish nature, and the hard, impassioned man poured his spunk deep into her belly.

Drabik had taken custody of the female when the lord of the manor had had his due. He led her to the pony barn where he accoutered her in her permanent ponygirl outfit: the blue, Neoprene hood, the heavy, black, leather boots, the hard, confining collar. And then he whipped her, her arms strung up above her, her legs clamped together tightly. He used a long, black, leather bullwhip that left dark, deep red wounds wherever it landed. It took a delicate hand to bruise the flesh without tearing it, but Drabik was a master with the bullwhip and only a line or two of blood trickled down the naked female's torso. When he was satisfied that the once human female had been terrorized beyond all endurance, had suffered enough pain to have branded into her being the fear of the lash, he released her, joined her wrists behind her back and forced her to her knees. He removed her shield gag and pried open her trembling lips with his rampant manhood. She understood at once what was required and she began to suckle the thick meat immediately, sobbing all the while. When he was ready, he plunged his cock deep into her throat and spilled himself there, pressing her lips against his belly while she gasped desperately for air, holding her head firmly by the long, blond skein of hair that emerged from her blue covered head. Immediately afterwards, he had taken her to the training paddock and begun her lessons in her new life's work.

The naked pony had regained some of its composure and Drabik released her from the chain that led down from the training armature. He removed her gag and allowed her to drink from a large flask of water. The liquid spilled from her lips and dribbled down her chest as she hungrily took of the sustenance. When Drabik removed the flask from her pretty, plump lips, the former woman opened her mouth as if to speak, undoubtedly to beg for release or mercy. Drabik slapped her fiercely across the face and stuffed the gag back into her mouth.

He pulled the whining, sobbing pony to the side of the broad, hard scrapple dirt track, and then pushed her to her knees on the neighboring soft, green grass. The afternoon light shone directly into her smooth, blue covered face, or where her face would have been, and he could detect her darting, black pupils through the tiny eye openings. There was a creature in there, one that didn't fully realize what had happened to her. She undoubtedly still thought of herself in human terms, prayed that this Golgotha was temporary, looked for some slight sign of humanity in the face of her tormentor.

Drabik knelt down in front of the pony and began to caress her plump, pale orbs. They were paler than the rest of her but for the little triangle between her thighs. Soon she would be a uniform hue. Creamy, high spf sun block was painstakingly applied to the bodies of the ponygirls of Northern European descent several times a day, for their chalk white skin was highly prized. The darker skinned, Mediterranean ponies and the growing number of Latin American females had a lush tanning lotion applied, giving them a deep, bronze skin tone.

The pony gave a slight whine as she felt her mammaries groped by the cruel man who had driven her to exhaustion. He had kicked her thighs apart when she had knelt, and he let one hand slide down her tight, firm belly to the crux between them. Her belly was naked now, and her hairless slit was unadorned. Tomorrow, after she had been made to run with the other ponygirls, she would be taken to a shack on the edge of the cluster of buildings that served the estate, strapped into a specially designed chair and have the heraldic emblem of the estate tattooed on the tender, flawless flesh, just above her loins. It was a yellow, rampant wolf, its paws poised to strike, its fangs bared from its snarling mouth. Under it, the motto of the estate, "Sub Hoc Signo Vinces" – "Under This Sign We Shall Conquer," would be inscribed in florid, blue lettering. Rings would be installed in her nose and through the lower parts of her labia. The thick, golden nose ring was for fastening her in her stall in the pony barn. The smaller, bright yellow metallic rings in her loins would carry small golden disks recording the name and crest of her owner. On her chest, above her breasts, in two inch high Cyrillic lettering would be tattooed her new pony name. Drabik had not decided on one for her yet. He would run her some more later while he thought about it.

Drabik slid his left hand over the female's lower lips and caressed them gently. The ponygirl shifted her hips as if to deny him access to her sex, but memory of her recent beating kept her otherwise still. Soon, the tender cleft between her thighs began to moisten and Drabik eased the hairless lips apart and entered her womb with his fingers. To everyone's surprise and amusement she had been a virgin when Grobgy had penetrated her and she still bore evidence of her deflowering on her thighs. Within a short time, Drabik had the ponygirl moaning with unwanted desire. She mewed as her passions rose and Drabik's hand became slick with her discharge. Her breath became labored and deep, her breasts tightened and her nipples became as hard as buttons. Her mewing became louder and staccato as she was drawn closer and closer to her climax. She leaned forward and began a long, deep moan. Her whole body seemed to contract and then shuddered as the first wave of her pleasure went through her.

"Mmmmmpf! Mmmmmmmmpf! Mmmmmmmmpf!" she called out from behind her sound stifling gag as her body defeated her will to resist the man's manipulations of her sex. "Mmmmmmmmmmmpf! Mmmmmmmmmmmpf! Mmm-mmmmmmmpf!" she continued, her soft, round shoulders bent, her head bowed, as her pussy contracted again and again around Drabik's thick fingers inside her.

When he was satisfied that her climax had subsided, Drabik rose and then knelt down behind the blue hooded, whimpering female. He pushed her torso forward until her forehead was on the bright green grass in front of her. He released his already iron hard cock from its den and pushed it between the engorged lips that surrounded her lush and juicy cunt. She gasped as he entered her.

The assassin closed his eyes as he enjoyed the tight, moist warmth of her canal. He stroked himself back and forth along the walls of the hot tunnel slowly. Training a new ponygirl always raised his lust high. Each one he had trained had been like a new creation for him, molding the body of what once been a free, independent, young woman into a creature slightly more than a beast. He had his hands on her broad hips as he sawed his cock back and forth, pushing himself deeply into the near virgin crevasse. He heard the tell tale signs of her reaching a new crescendo of pleasure and he let his own passions flow unrestrained. When he heard her call out her lust, and felt her cunt convulse around his needy manhood, he began to pound his hips into the back of the female's thighs. He groaned as he came, his cock jerking and pumping within her.

The pony's passage was still giving off little throbs as Drabik's cock detumesced. He enjoyed the mild, pleasant sensations. The pony was sobbing and her bound hands behind her back were twisting and turning in their confines. Suddenly, Drabik heard the sound of two hands clapping behind him. He turned, his softened cock slipping from its temporary berth. A tall, svelte, young, black haired woman, dressed in tight, black leather slacks and a white short sleeved blouse sat astride an elegant, black thoroughbred. Her hair was long and streamed around her shoulders as if it had been recently blowing in the wind behind her. Her loose blouse was cut with a deep 'V' neck and the edges of her generous breasts could be seen. It was Grobgy's beautiful, depraved daughter, Anya. She had a finely sculptured, graceful face with deep, brown eyes. Her mouth carried a hint of her inner cruelty. Behind the sweaty horse, a long leather strap leading from the pommel of Anya's saddle to a ring in her collar, was a naked and very exhausted looking slave girl. She had long, blond hair that was tied off behind her head, pale, grapefruit sized breasts and a pretty, but unhappy, face.

Female slavery had been revived in Kalikastan at the same time that ponygirl racing was reinitiated into the ancient country. For 600 hundred years, the raiding tribes of Kalikastan, closely related to the Cossacks, had brought back from the steppes young, beautiful, female captives until their depredations had finally been halted by the armies of the Russian Tsar in the late 17th century. The Tsar had outlawed ponygirl racing and brought an end to female slavery. But in 1991, when the writ of the Communist Party of the Soviet Union ceased to run here, the Russian gangsters found a place to spend their ill gotten millions without fear of governmental interference. The nascent democracy had been brushed aside and a Commission took power consisting of the leading Russian crime lords. If one could conceive of how the five Mafia families of New York might run that city if they could eliminate police regulation entirely, this was Kalikastan. But you had to imagine it on a grand scale.

And so female sexual slavery existed side by side with the institution of ponygirl racing. The slave girls differed from the ponygirls in that they did not spend their days hooded and gagged and they had free use of their hands. But they wore the same tattoos and disks. Some, depending on the idiosyncrasies of their owners, were outfitted with golden rings through their noses like the ponygirls had. Slave girls were allowed to speak, but only if spoken to, of course. While ponygirls were considered to have been deprived of their human attributes, slave girls were considered to be nominally within the human race. But still, they were property, had no real rights and did not qualify to be considered really as people. They were useful, subservient and almost always pretty.

The slave girl at the end of Anya's tether bore a tattoo of a coiled serpent on her belly. It designated the House which had trained her. Grobgy trained ponygirls on his estate and they all wore his insignia. But he picked up slave girls where and when the impulse struck him and none of the slave girls wore the yellow image of the angry, rampant wolf. On their nether lips they did wear the disks that denoted them as his property and they wore their slave names tattooed across their upper chests. This girl's name was Elena. She was huffing and puffing, trying to catch her breath, her eyes wet with unhappiness. Long, red stripes encircled her torso, evidence of a recent engagement with the business end of a whip.

Anya slowly stopped clapping when she saw that she had the killer's attention. "Good work, Anton. Breaking the new pony in right I see," she called out in Russian, her amusement obvious. Anya was fully used to the sight of rough men sexually acting out on the bodies of the ponygirls and the slave girls. She had grown up mostly on the estate. She had no personal reservations about it. She also had free use of the indentured females, hence the pitiable, blond young woman behind her horse.

Drabik had no embarrassment at what the gang lord's beautiful daughter had witnessed. Anyway, she had seen his dick many times. At the risk of his life, Drabik had taken Anya as a lover. They trysted frequently at an inn about thirty miles from the estate run by local peasants. Grobgy had declared his 22 year old daughter off limits to all men. Several who had tested his commitment to this policy were dissolving into dust somewhere out in the Kalikastani plains. Somehow, to his surprise, Drabik had never been caught. In fact, Grobgy had decided to make an exception. The old man, he was in his early sixties, was looking for a successor, someone who could hold together his criminal enterprise and protect his daughter from the cruelties which might be inflicted on her as the daughter of a gangster past his prime. He liked Drabik. He was tough enough and smart enough. And so he ignored, for now, his daughter's coitus with his hired hand.

What Grobgy didn't know, he had been squeamish about bugging the bedroom that Drabik and Anya used, was that Drabik and the pale skinned, black haired, young woman had begun to play some pretty rough games together.

It all started when Anya had become jealous of Drabik's attachment to one of the ponygirls he had trained, Lightning. She had egged Drabik on about his growing emotional involvement. Ponygirls weren't women, they were animals. Animals who you could fuck, true, but not a creature with which one should fall in love. You might as well fall in love with your horse. Drabik, who spent his whole life suppressing any real human emotion in himself, was mortified that Anya had discovered his developing weakness. At her urging, he beat and tormented Lightning unmercifully just before the spring racing season. Lightning was scheduled to be turned over to her driver for the duration and she would be unavailable to be used by anyone other than him during the ten week meeting. The pony suffered mercilessly at his hands. It had turned Anya on to watch him dole out punishment to the pony and then use her body callously. Anya, her lusts aflame at the spectacle, had challenged Drabik to someday 'fuck me like a ponygirl'.

In the weeks that followed, Drabik had taken Anya at her word. The first time he just tied her up and raped her mouth. Since then he had dressed her in ponygirl boots and a ponygirl collar and then bound her wrists behind her just like a real ponygirl. The last time they had met he had placed a ponygirl hood over her head. Anya had screamed and moaned her pleasure at being so roughly treated.

Drabik looked at the desirable young woman in the saddle. He seemed to be eternally at lust and his cock stirred as he recalled the delights of her flesh. He would not fuck her tonight. Tonight he had reserved for Lightning. The pony was going into the care of her driver in the morning and she would be unavailable to him until the fall tournament was over more than two months hence. But tomorrow was another day.

He stood and tucked his fleshy weapon away. "I'm happy that you enjoyed the show, Miss Grobgy," he told her. He always spoke formally to her in the presence of others. So far he thought that no one had ratted him out to Grobgy and he wanted to keep it that way. A too familiar repartee between him and the black haired beauty might give the game away.

"Let me know in advance next time and I'll sell tickets. I'm sure everyone would like to see the famous Drabik cock at work," Anya replied. Drabik looked around quickly to see if anyone had heard. Anya was pushing the outside of the envelope. As well she might. It wasn't she who would be wearing a bullet hole in the back of her head.

"I'm going to run her some more if you'd like to watch, Miss," he said loudly. His face carried a frown, a signal to the girl that he disapproved of her flaunting their familiarity.

"No, thanks," Anya answered. She nodded her head backwards at the tethered slave girl behind her. "I've got some plans. But I'll be looking forward to a demonstration of your prowess again soon."

The woman kicked the sides of her horse and the large black beast jumped into a trot. Behind it, the slave girl's body jerked forwards as the tether connecting her to the saddle's pommel tightened. She called out, "Ooooooooh!" and resumed a barefooted sprint behind her mistress.

* * * * * * * * * * * * *

Leaving her steed outside in the care of a groom, Anya led the still heavily breathing, naked slave girl, Elena, through the broad oaken doors that served as the entrance to her father's mansion. The doors fed into a large entranceway with solid oak floors and a long, broad, curving staircase that served the upper levels. The stairs were carpeted with a thick, plush, red rug, and her boots were silenced as she trod upwards, the poor naked and bound slave girl in tow. Anya proceeded to her own luxurious bedroom and shut the heavy, solid door behind her. The male servants all had hidden knowing smiles as she had passed them. The slave girls who populated the mansion averted their eyes and tried to shrink inside themselves; none of them wanted to be the focus of the cruel woman's attention.

Anya's bedroom was decorated finely with a soft, heavy pile white rug and finely carved white oak furniture. She had a large four poster bed. She had specially designed the accouterments of bondage that decorated it, with easy to use rings and lamps installed in the head and foot boards and along the sides. Shiny brass railings ran along the top of the posts and across the bed, ready to assist in the proper positioning of a victim of her lusts for whipping or other torment. A series of three small cages lined one wall. Presently, only one unfortunate female resided there. She was bound and hooded in her tiny prison. Plugs in the hood excluded all sounds made in the room from her awareness, but she could detect the firm, deliberate footfall of her mistress through the vibration on the floor. Maliska, as she was now called, was Anya's body servant and saw to all her mistress's bodily needs. She was a thin, sleight young woman, with long, brown hair that fell to her waist. Having been fed and allowed to ease her bladder a short while ago by one of the male servants, she would be satisfied to be left unnoticed in her cage for as long as possible.

Anya had no thoughts for Maliska at this time. She was still focused on the pretty Elena. She dragged the sweaty and dusty young woman to the corner of the room. Anya had had the workmen install some special equipment there for her and dangling down from the ceiling was a series of long steel cables with metal clamps on the ends. Anya unlocked Elena's hands from behind her back and joined them again in front. She closed the clamp at the end of one cable to where the bracelets joined and activated the electric winch, which reeled the cable in. Elena's hands were slowly raised above her head until she was just able to touch the soft, fluffy carpet with her big toes.

"Did you enjoy your exercise, Elena?" the tall, lithe, gangster's daughter asked her in English. None of the slave girls were taught Russian. English, a common enough language in the outside world, was the *lingua franca* of the slave girls. Those who did not know it when they were enslaved learned it fast.

"You've gotten a little tubby lately, Elena," Anya said to the distended slave girl mockingly. "We need to work those fatty pounds off." Anya didn't expect an answer to her statement. The slave girl was too terrified to speak.

Anya stepped over to her tall, finely carved bureau and pulled open a drawer. She removed a blue, Neoprene hood and stepped back to the dangling slave girl. "I think I know what you need, Elena," Anya said tauntingly. "I think that maybe we'll make you into a ponygirl. Then you can run, run, run all the time. You won't have an ounce of fat on you. Would you like that?"

Elena, like all of the slave girls, was frightened whenever she saw the anonymous, hooded female creatures that lived down in the pony barn. Life as a slave girl was harsh enough. But to be treated like an animal, to be deprived of a face, a voice, the use of your hands, forever, that bespoke a horror too cruel to be contemplated. Elena marshaled the courage to speak.

"N,no, mistress," she replied timidly in a whispered, barely audible voice. "I wouldn't want that, mistress. Please."

"Oh, it might be good for you, Elena," Anya returned. She was standing a few inches from the helpless, young girl, twirling the blue hood in her hands. "All of that outdoor exercise would do wonders for you. And I'm told that they fuck almost all day long."

A wave of misery crossed the bound slave girl's face. Anya was known for her cruelty. All the slave girls tried to hide when she was around. Elena had been unlucky to catch her eye a few days ago and had been under a regimen of abuse and cruelty ever since. Her only hope was that the feared mistress would tire of her soon. But she would suffer anything rather than be turned into a ponygirl.

Anya took the hood and presented it to the young girl's head. "Let's see how you look, Elena," she said as she draped it over her blond hair. There was a hole in the back of the hood for the ponytail, but Anya didn't bother with that for now. She tugged the soft, pliable fabric over the girl's head and down over her face. The hood had an opening for her mouth, but covered her chin and went down over her neck. Elena gave a slight whine as her eyesight was diminished to what she could see through the tiny holes.

Ponygirl collars had little hooks that captured the eyelets in the bottom of the hood so that it could be pulled tight over the pony's face. The slave girls wore collars too, but they were not designed to be worn with a ponygirl hood. Anya let the bottom of the hood rest over the brass collar that Elena wore. She stepped back.

"Oh, Elena," she said playfully. "It fits you perfectly. Put a gold ring through your nose and you'd fit right in."

Elena's lips, the only part of her face that could be seen, were trembling. "P,please, mistress. Please don't make me a ponygirl! Please!" she cried out desperately.

Elena didn't realize that she would, in fact, not make a very good ponygirl at all. She was too short by about four inches and she lacked the broad back necessary for pulling a heavy pony cart. Her legs were short and graceful, not nearly well developed enough to provide the speed and strength she would need. While her breasts were full and ample, to be a ponygirl you needed breasts that were heavy and large. Of course, that had nothing to do with the functionality of a ponygirl, big breasts did not contribute in any way to strength or speed. But it was an issue of style. No one wanted to watch small breasted, naked, former human females running around a track.

Anya leered at the naked, hooded female in front of her. She was looking at Elena, but she was seeing Lightning. She hated that pony with an intense passion. If it were up to her, she would make it suffer every day. But she was one of her father's prized ponies and she didn't want to incur his wrath. Also, she knew that Drabik might punish her by depriving her of his presence and his thick, hard cock if he found out that she was abusing Lightning. He didn't give a fuck about Elena. And if she couldn't whip Lightning every day, she could whip Elena.

Anya had dared to take Lightning out for a ride one day when Drabik was away. She had whipped her unmercifully, tied to a tree deep in the woods that neighbored the estate. And she had caused Lightning's lover, another pony called Persephone with which Lightning had raced for a part of last season, to be sold. Anya was delighted as she had forced her hated rival for

Drabek's affections watch as Persephone was loaded onto a pony trailer and driven away. Tomorrow, Lightning would be out of her reach. She would be placed into the hands of her driver for two weeks of intense training and then for the length of the ten week fall season. Only he could touch her. But what made Anya really boil was the knowledge that tonight her lover would visit Lightning in the pony barn and fuck her. Probably several times. While she, Anya, a real woman, not an animal, would be alone in her own bed, but for the services of a female slave.

Her ire building inside her, Anya knelt down and linked the brown leather bracelets that surrounded the slave girl's ankles together. She then went back to her dresser and retrieved a thick leather gag. Unceremoniously, she presented it to the girl's lips and filled the slave's mouth. The outer gag was wide enough so that it covered the whole of the girl's lips and chin. Her whole face, but for a small space for her nostrils, was now hidden away. Anya went to the wall and selected a long, thin riding crop from the instruments of punishment mounted there. She swished it through the air. The slave girl's body stiffened at the tell tale sound. She uttered a mewing sound from behind her gag.

"Let's see if you can take a whip like a ponygirl," the cruel mistress told her. Anya reared her right arm back and let the whip fly. It landed across the unprotected, pale breasts of the helpless girl. A loud 'crack' resonated through the room. The girl responded with a low "Mmmmmmm-mmmm!" that emerged from her gag, a sound that would have undoubtedly been much louder were it not stifled by the thick plug of leather in her mouth. A bright line of red rose on the tender flesh. Anya smiled with satisfaction.

The poor slave girl writhed and moaned as Anya belabored her body with the whip. Again and again she laid the hard leather across her, striking her thighs and belly as well as her breasts. Long, angry red lines arose, overlaying the faded evidence of her most recent abuse that still lay there. Her naked feet hopped and danced, her hips writhed, her delectable breasts jumped each time the wicked instrument of torture met her tender skin. The chain that held the slave girl's hands aloft was positioned far enough away from the corner so as to enable Anya to move behind her and strike at her back and rear. "Oooooooooooo! Ooooooooooooompf" the girl cried out as her 'punishment' continued.

When Anya finally halted her assault, the slave girl was sobbing, her chest heaving, causing her pretty, red lined breasts to sway and jiggle. Anya's lust was on her now. She tossed the whip aside and leaned over, seizing the fleshy mounds with her hands. She placed her lips on the girl's nipples, first one and then the other, tasting the salty sweat of the girl's fear, licking and biting the stiff buttons. Anya stepped back and quickly tore off her clothes. Her own nipples were tight and hard with her passion. Her black, fur shrouded slit was plush and wet with her desire. When she knelt down to release the slave girl's ankles from their confinement, her large breasts swayed. Anya took the slave girl's right ankle and raised it up. She affixed it to one of the other chains that dangled from the ceiling. She then did the other. These chains were spread apart from the central one holding the girl's braceleted wrists and so the young girl's thighs were forced open, making available the appetizing female flesh between them. Anya caressed the hairless lips that surrounded the girl's sheath until the girl's moisture began to flow.

As a properly trained slave girl, Elena had, once her mistress's desire was known, taken her mind to a special place where she could release her own passion. Many sessions with the whip had taught her to bring herself to lust at a master's command. Elena had not had many opportunities for sexual adventure in the small, Norwegian fishing village from whence she came. There had been a boy, Herman, who she had liked. In the summer before her taking, she and Herman had taken the opportunity to slip away into the woods whenever they could. She had surrendered her virginity to him in a small, deserted cabin, lying atop a bed of grass and leaves that they had made together. It was Herman's youthful cock that she thought of now, how, after the first few couplings over that summer had put their youthful fumblings behind them, he had loved her tenderly and long, each time waiting for her passions to crest before spilling himself inside her.

It was only a few days after Hermann left for the University in Oslo, walking home late at night from her job at the local tavern owned by her uncle where she worked serving the hard but friendly fishermen steins of rich, golden hued ale, that she had been seized from behind. Tape covered her mouth as her hands were locked into hard, cold, steel handcuffs and a hood had been pulled over her head. The docks were just across the dark, lonely street, and she felt herself quickly dragged there. There was barely an opportunity to struggle. She was thrown into a boat, the engine roared to life and it pulled away. There was a pinprick in her right thigh and she lost consciousness. When she awoke, she was naked, bound and gagged, the hood still over her head. A few days later, someone came and took her away to Kalikastan.

Elena was grateful when she felt her assailant's fingers glide easily into her tender shaft. She felt the mistress's thumb tease her pleasure nub and a wave of lust coursed through her. Elena wanted her lusts to build, yearned for the throes of passion to overwhelm her. She had earned her pleasure with her pain and she wanted it.

Anya paused in her ministrations to the slave girl's cunt to run her soft hands over the girl's thighs and tattooed belly. She saw the sign of the girl's nascent pleasure glistening between her hairless nether lips. The aroma of the girl's excitement enthralled her. She walked over to the cages along the wall and released the slave girl Maliska, removing her hood and gag but leaving her thin wrists confined behind her. She pulled the girl over to where Elena was posed in the corner and instructed the brown haired girl to lie on the floor on her back, her head towards the other, suspended slave girl. She placed her knees on either side of the obedient head and nestled her leaking sex over the slave girl's mouth. The curly black thatch of hair that surrounded her cunt brushed across the yielding slave girl's face. The girl knew what to do without instruction, and she ran her well trained tongue over the outer lips of Anya's sex and then began to tickle the hardened pleasure bud that adorned their apex.

"If you make me come before I'm ready, cunt," Anya told her, her voice husky and thick with desire, "I'll whip you until you bleed."

Maliska shuddered at the thought. She would be cautious in her obeisance to the mistress's lush sex. She would be well attuned to her responses. Maliska, to her dismay, had been Anya's body slave for almost a year. She knew her mistress well and had practiced her cunnalinguist arts on her countless times. And she knew that Anya's promise to beat her unmercifully was not an empty one.

The girl worked carefully as the fecund odor of Anya's discharges overwhelmed her. Her own sex began to yearn for attention and she spread her legs in an almost automatic response. She regretted her bound hands behind her, yearned for the freedom to serve her own desire. She struggled not to lose herself in the magic of her mistress's pussy. The mistress was not always cruel and she had often had her mistress's head between her own thighs as she serviced the gangster's daughter. The afternoon was yet young and she calculated that she might still achieve her needs.

Anya moaned as she felt the tongue enflame her. Before her was the naked, hairless jewel belonging to the other slave and she pressed her head and tongue forward to take command of it. Elena moaned in turn as the woman's tongue delved deeply between her engorged lips and caressed her inner flesh. Anya's soft hands were on her tender, white, inner thighs and the heat from them drove her lust higher.

The gangster's daughter took her time drinking in the musky flavor of her slave girl's fecund pussy. She drove the suspended girl to the crest of pleasure again and again, only to draw back to let her cool. Elena shuddered in her need and murmured muffled imprecations to her assailant to allow her completion. Anya pressed her pungent sex down upon the mouth that serviced her. She felt her own breasts hard and needy, her points hard and almost aching. She seized the drooping orbs and caressed them, luxuriating in the pleasurable sensations.

Three times, poor Maliska, a former Hungarian shop girl, ceased her agitation of her mistress's hot crevasse when she sensed her reaching her climax. She could tell from the pressure of the woman's thighs against her cheeks, the panting of her breath, the groans of pleasure emanating from the mouth buried in the other slave girl's slit. Finally, Anya began to rock her hips against Maliska's mouth. Her hands went down to her forehead. "Yes! Yes!" she moaned. "Do it now!"

Maliska began to gemauche Anya's hot, moist cunt in earnest even as Anya seized Elena's bud of pleasure with her lips and sucked on it hard, teasing it with the tip of her hardened tongue. Elena felt her orgasm coming at long last and she moaned deeply behind her gag. Her thighs shook as her convulsions began and she called out, "Mmmmmmm! Mmmmmmmm! Mmmmmmmmmm!" as the stream of pleasure overwhelmed her. Anya was coming too, and she buried her face in Elena's lap, wrapping her arms around the girl's suspended and widespread thighs. "Oooooooooooh! Oooooooooooooh!" she yelled, raising her head for breath, calling out to the mouth that was tormenting her fevered slit. "Yes! Yes! Yes! Suck my pussy you slut! Suck it hard!"

Maliska's cunt burned with need as she took in the sound of the other women's orgasms. She pressed her thighs together in an attempt to squeeze her nether lips into pleasure as she obediently took her mistress's hardened clit into her mouth. Anya screamed her pleasure into Elena's cunt.

When Anya's throbbing orgasms subsided, she pushed herself off of the obedient head and rose to her feet. Elena was still moaning faintly. Anya studied the anonymous, blue clad head for a moment and then reached down and closed the Velcro tabs that sat just above the tiny eyeholes. Elena was deprived of light, but she didn't mind. She wanted to bask in the afterglow of her climax and to try and recall better days when her lover would have laid there beside her, murmuring his love and affection.

Anya walked over to a side table and removed a small glass and a bottle of vodka. She poured herself a large shot and downed it in one gulp. Her whole body was atingle from her orgasm. She wasn't finished. She ordered Maliska to rise and to get on the bed. The petit slave girl obeyed quickly. Anya had turned back the sheets and the small girl slid her body over the silk surface and lay with her back against the large, fluffy pillows, spreading her pale white, graceful thighs in anticipation. She watched as Anya took a large, thick, black dildo from the nightstand drawer and strapped it on. It was the one with the vibrating motor. It was Maliska's favorite. As Anya crawled onto the bed, lust in her dark, black eyes, Maliska wetted her lips in anticipation.

* * * * * * * * * * * * * * * * *

While Anya was playing with her toys, Axmail Grobgy was watching the final workouts of some of his ponies. Tomorrow morning they would all be sent to the camp on the other side of the estate, nearer to the grandstand and racing track where the actual contests of the fall meet would be run. There, in the custody of their drivers, they would spend the last two weeks of training. One of Grobgy's favorites, Lightning, was now running around the far turn in her first lap. Grobgy had his right boot up on the bottom rail of the fence that surrounded the training track and was standing next to the timekeeper. Next to him was the pony's current trainer, a short, thin man, fortyish, with long grey hair that was clipped into a ponytail behind his head. Next to Grobgy, on his right, stood the dwarf, Jerzi Gromyko, who would drive the pony this fall as he had done last spring.

"I still don't know why you switched her to the 3000 meter," Jerzi said to Grobgy, his expert eyes zeroed in on the racing pony's form through a pair of small binoculars, custom built for his size. "She beat all comers last year. She would be a cinch to do it again."

Grobgy took his eyes off of the pony Lightning for just a moment as he considered the dwarf's objection for the umpteenth time.

"It's settled Jerzi. She runs the 3000. I have my reasons. First of all, the pony that ran the 3000 for me last year is a year older. I don't think that it has the stamina to bring home the gold in the 3000 this year. I've slotted it for the 1500. She probably won't win, but she'll medal. Second, Lightning has been growing stronger every week as she did last year. She's at her peak. She may not win the first few races, but by midseason, she'll be unbeatable. Third, she's my pony and I'll do what the fuck I want with her."

The last comment was stated in the cold, harsh terms Grobgy used when he meant to terminate debate.

Lightning was coming around the near turn now and all eyes were on her. Her long, strong legs were pumping rapidly, each stride matched by a swaying of her ample breasts. Her body glistened with sweat and her black boots were covered with the dust of the track. Behind her, on the tiny sulky cart, sat her teenaged training driver, the smallest youth over 18 years of age that they could find. Ponygirl racing was a highly regulated sport and no one under 18 was permitted to go anywhere near the former human females. In an otherwise lawless society, this was an anachronism, but, after all, ponygirl racing was a sport of gentlemen.

Lightning ran by the group of men at top speed. She grunted through her bit with each anguished stride. The driver cracked the whip on her back, a measure totally unnecessary, since Lightning was already giving her all.

As the blue hooded pony began her second lap, the men all inspected the timepiece and nodded to each other in satisfaction. A seven minute, 6 second lap. It was just an average time for a world class 1500 meter run, but this was for the long haul and the driver was keeping a good pace so that the pony would have something left for the second lap.

Jerzi, being an irascible, persistent sort, went right back at Grobgy.

"I didn't sign on to drive a second rater. You know I was counting on another gold medal this year. And this year I could go head to head against my brother, Giorgi. He's driving the 1500 for the American. It's not fair."

Grobgy gave the four foot tall dwarf a death look. "You signed a contract with me to drive Lightning. The contract didn't say anything about what race she would run. You'll ride her and win. Just remember, it would take half as much time to dig a hole for you out on the steppes somewhere as anybody else. I'll get another driver if I have to, but you'll be eating dirt."

This was not an idle threat. Jerzi realized that he had pushed the ruthless gangster too far. He decided he better make up. "Ok, Ok, I didn't mean anything. I was just upset that's all. I'll drive that pony into the ground if I have to, but I'll get you your gold."

Grobgy smiled. It was an evil smile that sometimes presaged disaster for its target. But, luckily for Jerzi, not this time.

Lightning was running the back stretch. Several other men had grouped themselves along the fence to watch the spectacle.

The late afternoon sun was beating down hard on the straining pony. Lightning knew that something special was going on by the way that her driver was pushing her. She had seen the men at the rail, including her dwarfish tormentor from a few months ago. She also knew that she was being trained for a much longer race than last spring. She didn't have any inkling why. No one had told her and no one ever would. It was not something a ponygirl needed to know. All she had to do was obey and run like her life depended on it.

Her lungs were near to bursting and he legs ached. Her fists, at the end of her useless arms bound behind her back, were clenched tightly. The cart seemed to get heavier and heavier as she went on. But she was drawing on every ounce of strength she had. They could beat her, abuse her, do anything they wanted to her. But she was a champion. She reveled in that fact. She wore the gold disk on her collar to prove it. Being the best, running to the cheers of the crowd on racing day was to her everything now. Even more than the attentions of her former trainer, whose physical attentions she craved and desired. If she had to be a ponygirl, she wanted to be the best.

All eyes were glued to her straining form as Lightning rounded the final turn and came into the home stretch. The men could hear the crack of the lash as it bit into her back and rump, the cries of the driver as he urged the pony on. As she drew nearer, they could hear the footfalls of her tall, black, ponygirl boots striking the hard packed dirt of the track. Fifty meters, twenty five, ten, and then she crossed the finish line. The timekeeper, a wizened old fellow, short, but with a broad back and large, scarred hands, clicked the timepiece as Lightning's hooded head crossed it. The men looked at the watch. 13 minutes, 45 seconds! A very good time! Grobgy slapped the back of the timekeeper as if he had something to do with it. "Bravo!" he yelled. He turned to Jerzi, who also looked pleased.

"Well," Jerzi said, "maybe you're right after all."

The men watched as Lightning finished her cool down laps. Her driver brought her to the track gate where Grobgy, Jerzi and her trainer joined her. The young driver jumped off of the cart beaming. Grobgy congratulated him with a powerful slap on the back and then approached his prize ponygirl. Her body was awash with sweat still streaming from her pores. "Good little *Molnya*," he said to her in Russian as he stroked her strong shoulders and then took hold of her firm, large breasts. The blue hooded pony pointed her tiny eye holes at him. She felt his large, coarse hands cover her mounds and then pull gently on the fleshy protuberances at their tips. "Good little *Molnya*," he cooed to her again. *Molnya* was the Russian word for Lightning. The ponygirl, through the intercession of a kindly old groom one night, had learned the meaning of her name and she reveled in it. She also knew the face of her owner and appreciated his attentions. So long as she was valuable in his eyes, her life would remain relatively unchanged. Should she fall from favor, who knew what might happen? He had comforted her one night after her trainer, Drabik, had beaten her unmercifully.

The pony's hairless slit began to moisten automatically as the large, rough man caressed her breasts. Almost any physical contact excited her as a possible prelude to her use. Besides running, it was what she lived for.

Grobgy moved his calloused hands back to her shoulders and exerted a gentle pressure. Lightning knew what was wanted and she gracefully sank to her knees, the strong, thin traces still leading back from her leather harness, the twin wooden poles that led from the cart still connected to her hips. She watched as the big man freed his thick cock from his pants. It was already hardening. Grobgy reached behind her blue hooded head and released the leather covered, steel bit from her mouth. She spread her lips widely to test the freedom of her mouth and leaned forwards. She captured the head of Grobgy's cock between her lips and suckled at it softly. She felt his hand take a firm but gentle hold on her long, auburn colored ponytail and she felt the thick, hard meat slide easily into her mouth.

Lightning didn't mind the presence of the other men as she worked diligently to bring her owner to pleasure. To her, his public adornment of her mouth with his cock was as much a badge of honor as the gold disk that she wore attached to her collar. The men would see how he valued her.

The kneeling, dust covered ponygirl lost herself in the sensation of the salty meat. She ran her tongue over the glans and slid her lips down along the steely shaft. Her own passions rose as she ministered to him, hearing him moan with pleasure at each long, deft stroke. She pushed her faceless head into his belly, taking all of his long manhood into her, pushing the plump, rounded head of his prick into her throat. Grobgy had both of his hands on her blue clad head and was urging her back and forth at a pace that suited him. She issued her own moan as the slit between her legs burned with desire.

The man's grip became harder and his body shuddered. His pumping of her head became more urgent. Lightning made sure that each time her head was pulled back and pushed forward that her lips gripped the shaft tightly, that her tongue teased the tube of hard meat.

When his cock began to pulse and spasm inside her mouth, she readied to receive his spunk. Grobgy groaned mightily as he came, spewing his creamy load inside her. The ponygirl relished each drop of her reward, drinking down the discharge as if it were nectar. "Ohhhhhhhhhhh!" Grobgy groaned one last time and he shoved his cock deep inside her throat. He held her there, her throat pierced by his hard, throbbing flesh until its convulsions subsided.

Smiling with now doubled satisfaction, Grobgy withdrew his softening manhood from the pony's lips and patted her on the head. "Good little *Molnya*," he repeated softly.

The gangster buttoned his cock back into its cave and turned to the other men. "Come on," he said to them. "Let's go have a drink."

CHAPTER TWO
A VISIT TO THE PONY BARN

Michael Burnham, the American billionaire, slammed his phone down into its cradle. He was not a man who took bad news well. And he had just received some very bad news.

Burnham was the master of a large estate in the Kalikastan hinterland, an anomaly among the mostly Russian criminals who owned the forty or so major estates in the country. He had come into possession of the estate, and his honorary Kalikastani citizenship, by an unusual route. It had all started with the kidnapping of his favorite and only niece, Maddy, many months ago. She had disappeared one night on her way home from her evening classes at a rural Tennessee junior college. Burnham had wanted to pay for her to attend one of the prestigious Eastern universities, but Maddy wanted to go her own way, loved it in the South. She had moved there as a teenager with her father from Cleveland, and refused his noble gesture.

When Burnham had learned of her disappearance, he had hired a 'fixer' known as Jake Barnes, a man he had done business with before, to track her down. Jake had a reputation of getting the job done and not being too concerned with collateral damage. He had traced Maddy to a farmhouse in Georgia where he had learned that Maddy had been kidnapped on more or less special order. From there Maddy had been traced to a warehouse in Elizabeth,

New Jersey, which was the headquarters of a female slavery ring. By the time that Jake and his crew had broken into and taken over the warehouse, Maddy had long since been shipped off to Kalikastan to be converted into a ponygirl.

Kalikastan being an insular country made getting into and out of the country unnoticed virtually impossible. Jake had come up with a scheme where they would take over the slaving operation, make contact with the Kalikastani end and, essentially, bribe their way into the country. With the cachet of being fellow international criminals, Burnham and Jake were accepted into the Kalikastani underworld. Burnham used his contacts to win the award from a Western European governmental consortium for construction of a multi billion dollar oil and natural gas pipeline through the small nation and promised to spread freight car loads of cash all around. He had done such a good job of convincing the locals that he was one of them that, essentially, he became one of them.

Burnham had become enamored of the delights of female slavery and had moved his operational headquarters to the large, rural estate that the National Commission had awarded him. Now, he was busily building a small slave empire in the country, establishing his own training facility, making contacts with various international slaving groups and working hand in hand with the principal importer of female flesh, Rashid Khalid, through whose facility in the capital, Dlitski, virtually every enslaved female who came into the country passed. From there they were wholesaled out to various slave trainers or sold off to special buyers. Maddy had come through Khalid's facility, and it was there that she was converted to a ponygirl.

Once in the country, Jake had started a search for Maddy. He had disguised his quest through acting as a buyer of ponygirls for Burnham's estate. After several weeks on the road, going to estate to estate, viewing literally dozens of young, broad backed but nubile former females, he had identified Maddy at a racing meet. Since her face, like all the other ponygirls, was permanently obscured by a tight fitting Neoprene hood, he had to identify her some other way. He couldn't very well go up to her and ask her if she was Maddy Burnham. First of all, she wouldn't be able to speak, being constantly gagged, and secondly, if someone had overheard him and he had been caught, he would have been roasted over a slow fire.

But Jake had a picture of Maddy he had taken from her apartment in the initial days of his search for her. She was smiling, a free and careless smile, and was dressed in a very revealing bikini. She had a distinctive mole over her right hip. Jake had been on the lookout for that mole and, when he spotted it, and the girl matched Maddy's other physical characteristics as to height, hair color, general body shape, her knew that he had found her.

But when he conveyed the news to Burnham, Burnham had nixed a snatch operation. Rekidnapping Maddy, who had become the prized racing ponygirl Lightning, would cause all hell to break loose. Burnham didn't want anything to threaten his sweet setup in the country. He had moved to Kalikastan, as far as he was concerned, permanently.

And so another scheme was concocted. Jake recruited Jackie, an African American whore from Chicago, a beautiful, energetic young woman who he had helped out of jam once, to be brought to Kalikastan and made into a ponygirl. She had been a track star in high school before she had chosen the path of licentiousness. He promised her, on Burnham's behalf, a million dollars for her troubles and told her that she would be freed in about five months. As Jake understood it, once Jackie was properly trained, Burnham would challenge Maddy's owner, Axmail Grobgy, to a claiming race. If Maddy won, Burnham would grant Grobgy access to millions of dollars of graft from the pipeline construction. But if Jackie, now called Chocolate because of the color of her skin, won, he would get Lightning. They would then fake the death of the two ponygirls and sneak them somehow out of the country. Burnham had laid the groundwork for the bet after his 'tactful' effort to purchase the ponygirl champion had been rebuked at a celebration at the Grobgy estate following the spring racing season.

Now, Chocolate was in the final stages of her training before the fall racing season. She had developed into a real championship prospect in the 1500 meter sulky race, the division that Lightning had won a few months ago. But a spanner had been thrown in the works.

"Fuck!" Burnham yelled. The petite, naked, blond slave girl who was kneeling within arms reach of him behind his large, polished oaken desk trembled. She had seen the cruel American angry a few times and it never boded well for any female that was around him. She didn't mind servicing the large, muscular man, it was better than being a whore in the bunkhouse, but she had been at the business end of Burnham's lash a few times and wanted no part of it now.

"Fuck! Fuck! Fuck!" Burnham yelled. He picked up the phone and yelled into it, "Get me Irkut! And get Jake over here too!" He slammed it back down, went to his sideboard and poured himself several fingers of scotch. He threw it back and poured himself another.

When Irkut and Jake were admitted to Burnham's large second storey office in the estate mansion, the little blond girl was dangling from the ceiling by her ankles. Her hands were bound behind her and she was gagged. Broad red stripes covered her breasts and belly and the tops of her thighs. She was sobbing. She had short, curly hair and teacup sized breasts. She wore a tattoo of a snarling bear on her lower belly, the emblem of her training house. The Cyrillic letters tattooed above her pert breasts spelled, in Russian, her slave name, Isadora. Her hairless slit peaked out from between her joined thighs.

Irkut was Chocolate's trainer, and he had done a masterful job with her. She had been reluctant to give her all at first, for some reason Irkut didn't understand. But he had 'convinced' her that she had better forget a that she had once been a human female and remember that her usefulness and future depended on her giving herself over totally to her new role in life. Thereafter, she had pushed herself to her extremes of endurance and was turning in very respectable times.

Jake and Irkut took chairs in front of Burnham's desk. The billionaire still held the thick, leather covered crop with which he had belabored the flesh of the slave girl. His yellow Izod shirt showed evidence of his workout on her with large wet stains formed under his armpits. His brow was moist with perspiration. The girl was still moaning from her ordeal. Burnham raised his strong, right arm and let loose another blow across her thighs. "Shut up!" he yelled. Isadora gave a loud, tearful, "Mmmmmmmm!" in reaction to abuse to her flesh and then forcibly silenced herself.

When Burnham had seated himself back behind his desk, Jake inquired, ignoring the dangling, upside down, still lightly moaning slave girl, "So what's the big emergency?"

"I'll tell you what the big emergency is!" Burnham snarled. "It's Lightning, that's what it is!"

Irkut and Jake looked at each other. Irkut knew about the planned claiming race between Chocolate and Lightning, but was unaware of the real reason for it. To him, Burnham was a Western enigma. American billionaires were an exotic, foreign concept to him. If Burnham had become obsessed with owning Lightning, well, who was he to question it? He wouldn't be the first to become a little crazy over ponygirls. Who could blame him?

But Jake knew, of course, and he was prepared to hear the worst. This job had already taken months longer than Jake had anticipated and involved him deeper into the moral morass of female slavery than he had ever wanted to be. When he took over the Jersey slave operation for Burnham, he had envisioned getting in and out of Kalikastan as quickly as possible. So what if a few girls, who would have gotten snatched anyway, or if not them, some other girls, ended up in cruel, barbarous slavery because of his efforts? This was just collateral damage. He was proud of the fact that he always got the job done, whatever the cost. It was to be no different this time. But now he was in way over his head. He had been 'in country' for almost seven months. More than a hundred otherwise innocent, young women had passed through the Elizabeth warehouse during that time. He had, as befitted his role as a callous slaver, used the multitudinous captured and despoiled females who served as slaves in the God forsaken country as casually and, at times, as cruelly, as any one else. He even owned a slave girl now, one that had been given to him as a bribe for some unmentioned, contingent, future favor.

This was his second slave girl. His first, a buxom, blond haired young Dutch girl named Klara, had been stolen from him a few days ago. He had fallen in love with the beautiful slave and, had come to believe that she had loved him. Now she was gone, probably stolen by Anton Drabik, Grobgy's assassin, in an effort to force information from her about Jake's real plans in the country. He had met Drabik at Grobgy's party a few months ago and they had both recognized each other for what they were, ruthless killers. Drabik had refused to believe that Burnham's interest in Kalikastan was as benign as it seemed. So he had snatched the girl to see what, under the whip, she would tell him. Jake didn't know if she was alive or dead. But he had vowed two things. Never would he let himself get emotionally attached to a slave girl again. Dana, his new slave girl, paid the price for that vow now, daily. Secondly, he would get even with Drabik if it was the last thing he did. He would get this Maddy thing over with first, one way or another. Then he would hunt the Russian assassin down and kill him.

"So what about Lightning?" Jake asked. If Lightning was dead, he would go kill Drabik tomorrow.

"She's not racing the 1500!" Burnham yelled back. "I just got the information from the Racing Commission. Grobgy's entry list came out today and she's running the 3000 meter!"

"What?" Jake exclaimed. If the two ponies were running separate races, they could not meet in the championship. "Can't Chocolate run the 3000?" he asked.

Irkut spoke up. "Impossible!" he exclaimed. "She hasn't been training for such a long race. By the time she got used to that length, half the season would be over. She might not even make the cutoff for the tournament!"

Burnham didn't like to hear that things couldn't be done. He glared at the ponygirl trainer. "I thought you were the best," he spat at him.

Irkut's ire was up. "I am the best!" he retorted. "It just can't be done. Chocolate isn't a machine, she's an animal made of muscle and bone. Besides, we've already handed in our card. She's listed for the 1500 and you can't change that now."

Being a highly formalized sport, strict rules governed the registration of ponygirls for the racing season. Once a pony had been listed, only an injury would permit its replacement. Burnham, although this was his first racing season, wanted to field as full a team of ponygirls as possible. They had already listed a pony for the 3000 meter, a French pony named Nannette.

"Well, Nannette just got injured. We'll scratch her and replace her with Chocolate," Burnham said.

"Not if I have anything to do with it, Mr. Burnham," Irkut replied indignantly. "I have a reputation and I won't be part of it. In fact, I'd be honor bound to report it." Honor was an odd concept for men who enslaved and abused women for a living.

Burnham glared at the diminutive ponygirl trainer. Irkut had been in at the reintroduction of the sport in Kalikastan. Burnham had brought him out of retirement to train Chocolate. Burnham could always have Irkut killed. He had his own crew of Russian killers on his payroll now. But, he was well known; people might ask questions. He mulled over the possibility. There was deathly silence in the room.

Jake spoke up. "I've got an idea," he said. "I don't know anything about ponygirl racing, but couldn't we train Chocolate during the season to run the 3000 meter? She could run the 1500 in her regular races, but still be ready to challenge Lightning after the fall tournament. In fact, if we did it on the sly, we could pull a fast one on Grobgy. He wouldn't know that Chocolate was trained to run the longer race. We could take Lightning's driver by surprise."

The other men looked at Jake wonderingly. Irkut rubbed his grey stubbled chin with his bony hand. "Maybe," he opined. "It's never been done. It would be a lot of work for her. I don't know."

Burnham liked the idea. "We can't just pull Chocolate from the racing season. Grobgy won't race her if she's not seen as a challenge. But, if she wins the 1500, he'll be hard put to turn it down. People would say that he'd lost his nerve. I like it."

"You'd have to get her driver to go along with it. He might not want to risk losing the 1500 championship if Chocolate gets too tired out from all of the training," Irkut warned.

"I'll handle Giorgi," Burnham said. "I'll double the dwarf's salary." Money didn't solve every problem, but it solved a lot of them. "Besides, Giorgi will be pissed that he won't be able to challenge his brother Jerzi in the championship race. And he'll like the idea of putting one over on him."

The men all agreed.

Jake left Burnham's office in a deep funk. He had just condemned Jackie, now known as Chocolate, to three months of intense, painful training. He had heard about the dwarf Giorgi's reputation for handling ponygirls and he knew that Jackie would suffer the man's cruelest extremes to both champion at the 1500 meters and then beat the probable 3000 meter champion in a match race. But he had not promised her a rose garden. She knew that it would be difficult. On the other hand, who could really understand the cruel regimen under which ponygirls lived until he or she had seen it first hand. He had seen it, lived with it for many months and he still didn't believe it. Sometimes he wondered when the great charade would be over and all the ponygirls would take off their hoods and laugh at the big joke. And all the beautiful, naked slave girls would thank their masters for a wonderful time and take off for home.

It was Jake's concern for the brown skinned whore that had brought him to her stall in the ponygirl barn the night before. He had not made contact with her since she had been kidnapped even though he spent much of his time on the estate within a stone's throw of her. Irkut had discouraged contact since the pony had known Jake while she was still a human female. Total immersion in the ponygirl life was required for efficient training and a reminder of who she once was would be detrimental. A ponygirl needed to lose all contact with her prior life.

But knowing that the next morning Jackie would be turned over to the dwarfish fiend who would drive her impelled Jake to see for himself what she had become. He knew she had been fixed in her stall for the evening and he wandered through the warren-like passages of the pony barn until he found the 10' by 10' stall in which the former hooker was mounted. Since most of the ponygirls would be gone the next day, the barn was unusually busy.

He could hear the ponies in the other stalls being serviced by the horny grooms and trainers as they got their rocks off inside their charges for the last time for many weeks. The stalls were all numbered. Since all of the stalls were interchangeable, and the ponies of course had no possessions, the ponies were rarely kept in the same stall twice in a row. Jake had had to check the board near the entrance to the barn for Jackie's location.

The melancholy enforcer opened the swinging wooden door to Chocolate's stall and saw her standing at the rail that extended horizontally across the room at waist height. Her black booted ankles were spread wide and chained to hooks in the floor. The large, gleaming ring in her nose was tied off to a ring in front of her on the wall opposite the door. Her wrists were, of course, bound behind her. Her head was encased in the black Neoprene hood that was standard on the Burnham estate.

Chocolate heard the sound of someone entering her stall, but couldn't turn to see who it was. The chain to her nose was pulled taut, causing her to lean forward slightly. It had been a hard day of training. She had enjoyed the standard rubdown afterwards, the brief, but refreshing cold shower she had received. She had eaten her evening meal from a large wooden bowl on the floor from her knees. The groom had even given her a fresh hood, taking the sweat stained one she had worn all day away to be cleaned.

The sleek, strong, naked pony had no inkling that this was her last night in the pony barn for a while. She knew that her training was becoming more intense every day, but was happily unconscious of the fate that awaited her. She had noticed the unusual level of activity in the barn, the noise of her sister ponies being used all around her, but she attached no special significance to it. Many things happened around her that she could not understand. It was best for ponies to disregard anything that did not involve them directly. Whip avoidance had been deeply engrained in her. She would run, fuck and do anything else that she was ordered to do, and that was all she needed to know.

Jake had seen Chocolate running the track many times from afar. But he hadn't been able to get a close look at her. He remembered the elegant, voluptuous whore he had fucked in Chicago. While he recognized this flesh as belonging to the same creature, he was surprised at how much it had changed. Her thighs, always strong, were now heavily muscled. Her shoulder and back muscles were like rocks. Her sides were lean.

The pony's body shifted nervously in reaction to his presence. Ponies never knew whether the presence behind them intended to bring them pleasure or pain. The long, brown ponytail that emerged from the tightly fitting neoprene hood swung gently behind her as she moved her black clad head nervously, futilely attempting to gain knowledge as to the identity of the male who had entered her little world. The Neoprene hoods used on Burnham's estate were black to match his 'team' colors of black and gold. Grobgy's colors were blue and gold and so they used blue hoods on his estate. Other estates used red, green, yellow and so on.

Jake noticed signs of Chocolate's recent use. A long, slick stain ran down the inside of her right thigh. Someone had been there before him. He stepped over to the side of

the stall and placed a thick, long nozzle on the water hose.
He turned on the water and let it run until it was lukewarm
and then he rinsed the insides of the pony's thighs. He
placed the nozzle against her hairless nether lips and let the
force of the water wash out the remnants of the prior man's
discharge.

Chocolate knew that the washing of her loins was
prefatory to further sexual use. The nozzle pushed aside her
labia and the stream of water entered her, giving her a sense
of warmth that spread from her loins to the rest of her body.
She had been fucked three times already tonight, but had
not been allowed to come. She flexed her knees and
wiggled her rump unconsciously in anticipation of another
chance.

Putting aside the nozzle, Jake used a cloth to wipe the
pony's legs and pussy dry. He stepped up behind her until
he could feel the heat of her body. Back in Chicago,
whenever he was in town, Jackie would fuck him for hours
for free. He knew her body intimately. He placed his strong
hands on her shoulders and let his hands slide along her
smooth flesh. His pale white hands were in contrast to the
shiny, brown skin of the ponygirl. She had a kind of dark,
coffee color and he recalled her skin being sweet to the
taste. He ran his hands over her broad but graceful hips and
the pony shuddered. Her hands writhed needfully in her
bonds behind her, her pale palms facing outwards. Jake
took his right hand and let it pass over her firm rump, drag
over the brown star between her rear cheeks and descend
between her outstretched thighs.

Chocolate gave a little moan through her gagged mouth
as her fires started to burn. When Jake took possession with
his hand of her already leaking nether lips, she moaned

again and tried to meet his caress with her hips. Leaning against the horizontal wooden bar, her feet firmly anchored, her nose ring connected tightly to the wall in front of her, Chocolate had little room to maneuver. When she felt his fingers tease open her engorging crevasse a wave of lust passed through her. She didn't know, didn't care who the man was behind her. She wanted to be filled, to be brought to completion. She yearned for his presence inside her.

Chocolate had fucked hundreds of men before becoming a pony girl. Some were careful, considerate lovers, even though she was a whore. But most men used her like a rag, something to deposit their spunk into. And so she had learned to take charge, make the man adopt her pace, get what pleasure that she could. But since her dehumanization, the men had been in charge. And she had learned to accept it. She was surprised at the lust they were able to draw from her, how her pussy watered when touched, how her breasts filled, her breath grew short. Every day, often many times a day, the men had made her come until she had begun to live for it, need it. Aside from the physical exhilaration she now felt at the end of a good, long run, or after a hard, driving sprint, it was the only pleasure she had.

But sometimes, like this evening, they ignored her needs and merely satisfied their lusts upon her. And so she was charged with passion now, hungry for the feel of a fat, hard cock plowing her needy channel.

Jake was hard and he withdrew his cock from his pants. The pony stiffened as he ran its rounded head along the lines of her slit. Jake teased her pussy, pushing in slowly until the helmet of his piece was enveloped by the fleshy folds and then withdrew. Each time, he pressed inside her a little farther, only to ease himself back out. Chocolate's ass jumped and ground in frustration. She gave a long, plaintive moan. Finally, Jake plunged his cock into her depths until buried to the hilt. The pony gave a pleasured sigh.

Maintaining a slow, steady pace within the brown skinned, bound female, Jake took his hands and circled her torso until her heavy breasts were encapsulated by his palms. He remembered these delightful breasts well. A wave of pleasure flowed through him as the heat from her cunt baked his stiff rod. He squeezed the fleshy mounds softly, and then took hold of the hardened nipples and pulled and tweaked at them. The pony's breath was coming swift and hard. He felt her body shudder. The fire that had been lit by the other men now exploded in her and her moist, hot crevasse was gripped with convulsions. Jake felt each hard contraction on his tool and heard the ponygirl moan with pleasure, "Mmmmmmmm! Mmmmmmmmmmmm!" as her whole body shook. "Mmmmmmmmmm! Mmmmm-mmmmm!" Her ecstasy emerged as a loud, muffled rumble from behind her gag.

The impassioned man kept up at his strokes. He wanted it to last, to hear the whore come once more. She had used to call out loudly when she came, urging him on, calling the tune to his strokes. But now all she could do is issue garbled, muted supplications.

Jake felt Chocolate's passions rising again. His resolution to delay his own orgasm was being overwhelmed by his own fevered need. Again and again he plunged inside her. He felt his balls tighten, the exquisite ache that presaged his climax. He twisted Chocolate's fat nipples hard and the ponygirl seemed to jump in response. It was what she needed and her pussy's convulsions began anew.

Jake could hold out no longer and his cock began to throb and pulse inside the hot tunnel. His cum flowed like a river down his steely shaft and he groaned loudly, his eyes rolling back into his head, his brow furrowing, his face muscles clenched. "Arrrrrgh!...Arrrrrrrgh!...Arrrrrrrgh!" he yelled as his cock took control of his whole being. He felt his knees weaken and he leaned into the pony, pressing his lips against the brown skin of her back.

As his orgasm faded, Jake slowly recovered his rational self. He rubbed his hands along the broad, strong shoulders of the ponygirl and down around her chest, giving her heavy orbs a thankful, soothing massage.

Now, as he strolled across the vast, neatly trimmed lawn that separated the Burnham mansion from the carriage house where he and his boys lived, Jake's cock stirred in remembrance of his passionate interlude with the female he had known as Jackie. She was spending her first day at the ponygirl encampment and he wondered what cruelties she was suffering at the hands of the vile dwarf, Giorgi. He cursed himself for volunteering the scheme that would make her ordeal all that much harder. A sea of rage boiled within him and he knew that he had only one outlet for it.

When he entered the cottage, two of his men, Curly and Leon were seated in the kitchen eating a late lunch. The table was covered with plates and dishes and a tall pitcher of the hearty, local ale. Curly was feeding some scraps from his meal to a giggling slave girl who was kneeling on the floor next to him. Leon had another one on his lap and had in his tongue in her willing mouth, licking her tonsils. His hand was buried in her hairless quim. The activities ceased the moment he walked through the door.

Jake had been away when Klara was stolen and his men had been charged with looking after her while he on his trip. When he returned and learned that she was gone, he smashed every breakable thing in the kitchen, including the windows, overcome by rage and unhappiness, while his men stood around mute and ashamed at their failure and the slave girls cringed in fear. Since then, they had all given him a wide berth.

Passing through the kitchen wordlessly, Jake walked up the stairway to the second floor. His room was first on the left. It was the largest of the bedrooms and had a large king sized bed with a heavy, dark oak frame. The corner room had two banks of windows, one that looked out over the practice track and the other which had a view of the mansion. There was a large, walk in closet and a private bathroom. The dresser was made of the same dark, polished wood as the bed frame. The dark green rug was a soft, padded, round area rug that allowed the shiny maple floor stand to out. The only other furniture in the room was a side table that doubled as a liquor cabinet, a soft easy chair, a tall floor lamp for reading and a 3' x 3' steel cage.

Kneeling in the cage, her large, starry blue eyes peering out fearfully, was a forlorn, young, naked woman with long, black hair. She was wearing one of the shield gags over her mouth and chin.

Dana had been Jake's slave only for a few days, but she had learned to fear the dark, lean, muscular man. When he had first used her, before she had been given over to him after a big party Burnham had thrown for the Kalikastani upper crust in the capital, he had seemed nice enough, almost tender. It was the first American man Dana had come into contact with since her enslavement. Dana was from Ohio and had been attending college at the time of her capture. She had gone through the regular slave training, a harrowing and painful experience, but she had been bought by an easy going, almost jovial caterer to serve as a waitress and party favor at various functions in Dlitski. She had adapted to her new life as an owned whore quickly, if reluctantly, and her owner had hardly ever beat her during the four or five months that she had been his.

Jake had taken her to his room after the party and she had serviced him as skillfully and dutifully as she would have any other guest. She had been surprised when, the next morning, she had been taken away by him and transported to this remote estate deep in the Kalikastani hinterland. Since her arrival here, she had lived a frightful, terrifying existence. Her new owner had beaten her terribly upon her arrival and several times since. He kept her locked in this cage almost all the time. He used her brutally and callously, with none of the tenderness she had experienced that first night. She had watched, tethered and bound, when he had torn apart the kitchen downstairs on that first day. She had shivered and quailed with fear at the prospect of being this explosive man's property and her fears had been well borne out.

Although slave girls were not supposed to talk, one of the other slaves had, in a low whispered voice when freeing her from her cage to eat and use the bathroom, explained to her what had happened, about Klara, and how she had been stolen. She knew that she was paying the price for her owner's loss. If only she could talk to him, she thought, show him that she could be a good slave to him, maybe things would go better. She had been trained to give exquisite pleasure to men and she was ready to devote to him all of her skills if only he would let her. It wasn't that she was enamored of him; she hated all of the men who used her against her will. But she had learned that the only way to ameliorate her new, cruel life was to use her body as an instrument of pleasure, to be obedient and servile. Someday, maybe she could escape. But until then she had to live.

Jake took little notice of the apprehensive slave girl when he entered the room. He went to the side table and poured himself three fingers of gin. He tossed it back quickly and then poured himself another. He took a long sip and then turned to the girl in the cage. She looked pitiful, all scrunched up, her hands bound behind her. He had gone out of his way to make sure that Klara's life as his slave was as free from discomfort and unhappiness as he could. He never caged her, had whipped her only once and then had forsworn violence against her. He had lost his heart to the ever smiling, delightful blond beauty. It had posed him quite a dilemma. He knew that he would leave Kalikastan someday. And he knew that he wouldn't be able to take Klara with him. He had struggled with the thought of abandoning her to a cruel, uncertain fate. Well, that problem had been solved. And he would never let himself care about a slave girl again.

Dana's very fragility as she knelt in her tiny prison was a trigger for Jake's baser instincts. He looked at her now and his hatred for her helplessness and innocence burned within him. Who was she to look at him with those doleful eyes? Who was she to be so soft and pretty and desirable? Her very existence was a challenge to his sense of himself as a man who dealt out rough justice. If he could not help Jackie, or Klara or even Maddy, who was she to expect mercy from him?

Dana watched as the man drew off his clothes. She whined involuntarily through her gag as she anticipated his next move. She had been confined in her cage for many hours and her muscles were cramped and aching. She had yearned for freedom. But now, she viewed the tiny, steel prison as a haven of sanctuary, a place where the man's whips could not reach her. She didn't want to get out and face his wrath. But she knew that she would.

Jake tossed his clothes on the floor and stretched. He was of medium build, almost wiry, but his muscles had great strength and were finely demarked across his body. He carried the scars of several bullets on his shoulder and arms and the leavings of sharp, pointed objects that had been directed at him with hostility. He was no Adonis. But his body had a rough grace, his movements smooth and deliberate. He turned to the creature in the cage, ready to do his will.

The cage unlocked with the disconnection of two hasps on the sides and the front swung free. The slave girl looked up at him sorrowfully. "Get out," was all he said, his voice deep and morose. The girl's eyes watered and her body seemed to shiver. But she forced herself forwards at his command, edging her way past the doorway. When she cleared it, she remained kneeling over, afraid to do more in the absence of a command.

"On the bed," Jake ordered, and the frightened girl rose to obey. She moved slowly, needing to stretch the muscles of her back and legs. As soon as she could, she crawled up onto the plush, thick mattress. She knelt on it, her back straightened, her bound wrists behind her, her knees wide apart facing her tormentor. Her pretty, round breasts swayed slightly as she adjusted herself to her position. There was a hole in her stomach, one of fear. She tried to push her chest out, angle her pelvis upwards so that the man might view her delights and forgo abuse of her to possess them. She tried to make her eyes express voluptuousness to him, convey a promise of earnestness in bringing him pleasure. If her mouth had been free, she would have opened her delectable lips and smiled, in spite of her fear and loathing of him, offering the enticement of their use.

Jake was having none of that. Although he viewed the graceful curves of her body with lust, appreciated the firmness and plumpness of her breasts, he had his own agenda. "Lie down on your back," he told her gruffly. "Head towards the foot of the bed."

Dana complied quickly, distraught that her efforts at seduction had been of no avail. The mattress was covered with a soft, blue, cotton blanket. It was soft enough so that her bound arms behind her sank into it, assuaging the discomfort of lying on them. She looked up at the ceiling and drew a deep breath through her fear dilated nostrils. She spread her legs automatically.

"Farther down," Jake ordered sternly. "Put your head over the edge of the bed."

Dana pushed herself down towards the foot of the bed by her heels until the back of her neck met the end of the mattress, She let her head fall down so that now she had an upside down view of the room. Her long, black hair fell in a cascade beneath her. She sensed Jake moving towards her and then saw his loins presented in front of her face. His cock was long and thick and in the process of engorgement.

His thighs and chest were hairless, but a forest of brown, curly hair surrounded his sex. Jake leaned over and released the gag from behind her head. She was grateful for the freedom of her mouth and took a long, anxious draft of air into her lungs. She knew that the thick gag of leather that had filled her for so many hours would soon find its replacement in the hard, heavy meat of Jake's cock. She also knew that, her head poised as it was, that it would be the tight, constrictive entrance to her throat that he would seek. She parted her lips in obedient readiness.

Jake stepped away from the bed long enough to retrieve a 2' long, thin, leather covered reed from the wall. An array of instruments of punishment was mounted there for the convenience of guests. He had already used several of them upon the slave girl's flesh and her body still carried evidence of her mistreatment. He stepped back to the bed.

The mattress rested upon a thick box spring which raised the surface of the bed high from the floor. Dana's head was waist high to Jake and he placed his thighs in front of her. He took his hardening cock in his right hand and pressed the head of it against Dana's upper lip. He slowly circled her mouth with it, teasing the opening. His cock grew harder and longer as he did so, his balls resting on the subjugated face beneath him.

"Bend your knees and keep your legs wide," he told the slave girl. Dana obeyed quickly, knowing that she was exposing her delicate cleft to her master's depredations. She moaned in fear and her stomach grew tight. He was going to beat her pussy, she knew it and she yearned to close her legs to protect it. "Keep your legs spread," Jake told her in his deep, unkindly voice, "or I'll whip every inch of your body."

Dana, trembling with fear, lifted her knees in response. Jake walked to the front of the bed and took two pillows. "Lift your ass," he said. The frightened girl raised her hips into the air and Jake slid the pillows under her. He stepped back to the foot of the bed. Now, the hairless slit was raised high, its entire length vulnerable to his whip. His cock was rock hard and he slowly introduced it into the waiting mouth. Dana pressed her lips around the meaty shaft and circled the knob with her tongue. Her eyes were closed, but she could feel and smell the heat of Jake's loins on her face. Jake moaned as she used the moist warmth of her mouth to pleasure him. Her whole body trembled, knowing that shortly she would feel the sting of her master's whip between her thighs. She felt him tap the end of it lightly on her pleasure bud, a harbinger of what was to come.

Jake let the tip of his whip slide along the length of the girl's hairless slit. He rubbed it up and down her creamy thighs while he enjoyed the efforts of her tongue on his rod. He then raised the thin reed and brought it down hard, directly over the defenseless crevasse.

"Mmmmmmmmmmmmm!" Dana cried out, her voice muffled by Jake's cock. Jake felt the tremors of her protest vibrate through his pole. He struck again and the girl moaned loudly in pain. "Mmmmmmmmmmmmm!" Her thighs shuddered and her back arched, but she continued her ministrations to his cock.

Dana fought off the desperate urge to close her thighs to protect her tender pussy. Her hands squirmed behind her back. When the man struck once more, she gave out a heartfelt sob and tears began to flow down her face.

His heat growing, ignited by the girl's suffering, Jake pushed his cock further into his whore's mouth. He found the entrance to her throat and drove the fatty head of his prick past it. Dana coughed and moaned as she felt her esophagus filled with the steel hard meat. Another cruel blow landed on her now raw pussy and she gagged and whined in response. She dug her heels into the bed frantically. Her lungs began to ache from the lack of air. Finally, when the girl had reached the extreme of distress, Jake drew his manhood back until the slave girl could pull the needed oxygen into her lungs.

The girl sucked in the air gratefully. Jake watched as her pretty breasts, melted on to her chest in repose, shook and swayed in response to the her desperate breaths. Dana bore the tattoo of a snarling fox on her lower belly, the sign of the house that trained her, and it danced and shimmied as her stomach undulated in response to her agonies. Jake left the whip aside and placed his hands on the recumbent breasts. Massaging their pleasant, fleshy bulk, he began to saw his cock back and forth between the slave girl's lips. He groaned with pleasure as she gripped the shaft tightly with her lips and caressed it with her agile, well trained tongue. His balls were tightening now in readiness for his discharge. His brain began to tingle with anticipation of the ecstasy to come. He tweaked the hard, stiff nipples of the girl's breasts until she gave out another moan of distress. It was the signal his cock had been waiting for. It throbbed and convulsed in the girl's mouth as it pumped his spewm out into her.

Jake kept up the pressure on the peaks of the girl's breasts, causing her to moan and whine with pain. Her legs danced on the bed, her chest heaved, as the pain tore through her. Dana swallowed the flood of come dutifully while inwardly cursing the man who was tormenting her, praying that her ordeal would end.

When Jake's cock slowed its convulsions, and the last drops of his come were laid into the slave girl's mouth, he released the tender orbs and let his cock slide out from between her lips. A line of his slime extended from his cock to her mouth, and he let it descend across her face before pulling fully away.

Jake was pleased with the intensity of his orgasm and the enticing way that the girl had taken his blows. Her pussy was glowing red from its abuse. He could hear her crying, and he saw her tears streaming from her eyes, flowing down into her scalp, her long, shiny black hair draped like a curtain below her. He went to the sideboard to pour himself another gin. He shot back a double shot and poured another. His head swam with the intoxicating effects of the alcohol. He regained the whip in his hand and he landed a sharp blow across the unhappy slave's belly. She screeched in pain.

"Get up," he ordered churlishly. "On your knees, head down towards the front of the bed. We're not finished yet."

CHAPTER THREE
AN OLD FRIEND

There had been some dramatic changes in Lightning's life in the last 24 hours. Change was something always trepidatious to a ponygirl. There was something comforting in the daily routines of the pony barn. Every morning a groom or a trainer came to your stall, and after releasing you from your evening confinements, fed and washed you and then stroked or fucked you to climax. There would be the morning run with all the other ponygirls, dashing a lap around the practice track and woe betides to the pony that finished last. Then there would be a morning training run, lunch, more running and then evening. Sometimes, the ponies were released into the large, grassy, enclosed field next to the pony barn and allowed to wander its expanse, make strange love to each other, or sit in the cool shade down by the brook.

With small exception, such as whether this or that master deigned to use them for sexual release, the days were all the same. Even the long hours spent confined to their stalls could be comforting in a way. Although nothing could make you feel more like a beast than to be tethered for hours on end, your wants and needs ignored, isolated in a little world all your own, it was better to resign yourself to your status, better to forget that you were once a woman, that you had a past, that you ever were or could ever be free. The times of isolation in her stall gave a ponygirl the opportunity to sink deeper and deeper into her transformation. Bound into virtual immobility, poised at just the right angle for penetration, her thighs widespread, her labia parted, her smaller, rear hole exposed, left to contemplate the fruitlessness of resistance, the impossibility of escape, able to see only through her little eye holes the wall before her, empty but for the steel ring embedded there holding fast the chain that pulled her nose ring tautly forwards, a ponygirl learned to surrender to her new nature. She was at the mercy of her masters, and virtually had no existence except in the presence of one of them.

But change often meant a new trainer, whose demands and preferences one would have to learn all over again. Change could mean being trained to a new cart, from a four pony cabriolet, for instance, to the six pony landau. New running partners, a whole new pace, it might take many beatings until you got it just right. Or you could be sold, transferred to a new estate, new rules, new rigors. Or, for the older ponygirls, you could be retired, and none of the ponygirls knew what that meant. But if your usefulness as a ponygirl was over, what more use could they have for you?

For Lightning, change meant, this time, being delivered into the hands of the cruel pony driver Jerzi Gromyko. It meant being transferred to the ponygirl park near the tournament track and the grandstands. It meant being away from the only person who seemed to care for her.

Lightning had been aware that the racing season was to start shortly just by the fact of having seen the dwarfish form of her driver together with her owner watching her run on the training track. She had gone back to the barn that afternoon with a heavy feeling in her gut. She remembered well her driver's brutality to her. Standing, bound in her stall for what seemed like hours, having been fed and washed by a groom, listening to the sounds of the day to day hustle and bustle of the ponygirl barn, she prayed that she would see her trainer one more time before she was handed over to the demonic dwarf.

She was not disappointed. Late in the evening, after the sun had melted away and darkness had crept into her little stall, she heard the door open and close behind her and the sound of her trainer's heavy boots. She felt his thick finger trace a line along her hairless slit between her outstretched thighs. She could not turn to see him, but she knew from this gesture that it was him and her loins began to burn with anticipation of her use.

Drabik used her often, many different ways, but her favorite was when he drew off his clothes, laid her to the floor of her stall and let his hot skin make contact with hers the entire length of her body. So she was joyful when she heard the unmistakable sound of him drawing his clothes off, the sound of them falling to the floor, the removal of his heavy work boots.

The naked man stepped behind her, between her widespread, anchored legs, and pressed his chest and loins against her. His heavy, calloused hands scoured her belly and then cupped her plump breasts. He took her nipples in his fingers and pinched them firmly, sending a shudder of expectant pleasure through her body. She could feel the heat of his torso against hers and his already stiff cock grazed her imprisoned hands behind her and then lay nestled in the valley between her pale white rear globes.

Strong hands brushed past her cloth covered face and loosened the chain that held her nose ring tautly to the wall before her. Her head now free, Lightning leaned back against her lover, reveling in the heat of his flesh against hers. His rough hands massaged her aching breasts and she moaned with delight. Her fever was rising in anticipation of her use. Other than her freedom, something that she still occasionally yearned for, there was nothing she wanted more in the world than to be possessed by her former trainer's cock.

Drabik slid his hands down the pony's sides and along her long, outstretched legs. He unhooked her ankles from the rings in the floor and then, tracing the same course along Lightning's pale white outer thighs, over her broad hips and along her taut torso, eased the pony back from the bar against which she had previously been leaning and urged her to the floor.

The polished wooden floor of her stall was dusty and hard, but Lightning didn't mind. As she lay upon her back, atop her bound arms, she caught, in the dim light, her first glance of her trainer's impassioned face through her tiny eyelets. She raised her knees and spread her legs obediently, dragging her still booted feet across the floor. She moaned as Drabik knelt between her thighs and again as he leaned over and took one of her hard, distended nipples in his mouth.

Drabik's lips and tongue teased her firm nipple until all of her being seemed to be concentrated on the little point of flesh. The man's hips rubbed against her pale, widespread thighs and his steel hard manhood lay across her belly. He shifted his attentions to the other nipple and Lightning moaned deeply, shifting her hips in almost anguished passion. Then, she felt his mouth and tongue descend across her firm, fluttering tummy, caress the insides of her navel, and then brush across her lower belly.

When Drabik's mouth seized her hardened nubbin of pleasure atop her engorged, needy labial lips, Lightning's whole body shuddered. He sucked at the stiffened protuberance hard and Lightning groaned with pleasure. Rough hands pushed her tender, pale thighs wider apart and a tongue delved deeply into her moist, hot slit. She thrust her hips up at the mouth that tormented her, relishing each twist and turn of the hot tongue, moaning loudly through her gag as it lapped at her engorged lower lips, tickled at her button of pleasure.

Three times, the man drove the supine, writhing ponygirl to the brink of climax. Each time, sensing her building crescendo, he ceased his supplications. On the fourth time, when Lightning's lust fevered brain felt on the edge of implosion, he let her come. The pony bucked and shook as the fierce tremors and contractions coursed though her body. She bit hard down on the thick wad of leather that filled her mouth, banged her heavy boots on the floor, screamed her joy into her gag. Her pussy pulsed with repeated hard, mind wrenching seizures of pleasure.

When her orgasm had finished cresting, her body still awash with desire, the eager lips left her loins and she felt the man's body move upwards. A hardness pressed apart her glowing lower lips and she felt her trainer's cock slide easily inside her. The thickness and heat of the rigid pole sparked a wave of pleasure that flowed through her entire body. Drabik pressed his weight down on her and his chest crushed her blood filled, twin globes down against hers. She wrapped her strong, long legs around his thighs and pulled him deeply inside her.

Slowly, deliberately, Drabik sawed his rock hard meat along Lightning's hot, tight canal. She shuddered and cried out each time the relentless cock buried itself to its hilt within her. She groaned into her gag as the meat rasped against her pleasure bud. Gradually, Drabik's thrusts became harder and quicker. She felt his hard hands grab her face and she peered out from behind her hood to see his cold, steely gray eyes peering back at her. As her climax renewed, she cried out in joy. She felt her trainer's body stiffen and heard his rough, loud groan. "Arrrrrgh!" he cried out as his thick cock began to throb and pulse within her. She felt his hot seed splash deep inside her womb and she thrust her hips back at him feverishly, her orgasm washing anew all over her.

When the man's forces were expended, he lay his body down heavily atop hers. Her pussy burned with the afterglow of her pleasure. Her legs loosened their grip on his and she felt herself melt into the floor beneath her.

For a long time, the two lay joined. Lightning could feel the beating of her lover's heart as, she was sure, he could feel hers. The ponygirl was in bliss. She had hoped and yearned for just this and it had come true. When the man's detumesced member finally slid free of her dilated slit, he eased himself off of her and lay by her side. Tenderly, he ran his hand over her hooded, anonymous, featureless head. Lightning cooed in appreciative response, the closest thing to a verbal communication that she was capable of. The rough, scarred hand stroked her breasts and belly lovingly. He dipped his hand between her thighs and covered her leaking, lush mons, gathering their commingled moisture. He brought it back to her ringed nose and she drew in the musky odor of her passion mixed with his. Her mind reeled at the scent and she looked at her lover through the tiny holes of her hood. "If I could only speak," she thought, "what would I say?" Would she say that she loved him? How could that be? He was her oppressor, the man who had stolen her womanhood from her, made her into the beast that she was. But she had never desired anyone as she desired him. The places where their flesh met along her long flank, the contact points between his hands and fingers and her tingling skin burned with electrified charges.

Drabik took the ring in the front of the ponygirl's collar and lifted her up until she sat next to him. He caressed her blue clad head, stroked the long, chestnut tail that sprouted from her blue covered head and then reached behind her and released the clasp that held her gag firmly in her mouth. He pulled it slowly free until Lightning's lips were liberated. She licked them anxiously. Her urge to break the ironclad rule of silence of a ponygirl had never been greater. It had been so long that she had formed words, used her voice, that she hardly remembered how. But she realized quickly the reason for her lip's liberation. Other than eating, there was only one use for a ponygirl's mouth.

The ponygirl trainer lay back and spread his legs in anticipation of the pony's obeisance to his maleness. Lightning rose to her knees and bent down until she could smell the musk of his loins. His long, thick tool was still flaccid, recumbent from its earlier toil. The pony brought her lips to the soft meat and subsumed its plump head into her mouth.

Drabik gave a sigh as the ponygirl's mouth began to excite his still soft cock. Lightning maneuvered herself between his hairy, outstretched thighs as she ran her tongue under the fleshy helmet and then drew it across the tiny hole at its tip.

It did not take long for the limp flesh to begin to engorge. Bent over, her firm, plump breasts crushed against her knees, Lightning moaned with pleasured satisfaction as she felt the hardening sword of flesh begin to rise. She could not speak her need for her former trainer, still her master like all the other men. But she could use her skilled lips and tongue to communicate to him her passionate union with him.

Lightning, her eyes closed behind her tight, blue hood, blissfully expressed her adoration for this man, her one, true master. She felt the tube of flesh hardening in her mouth, filling her oral cavity, its salty girth serving as her reward for her efforts. When the shaft stood hard and tall, she let it free and ran her lips down the length of the steely rod. Drabik moaned with pleasure as her tongue tickled its gnarly surface and moaned again when she enveloped the tight, scrotal sac beneath it, teasing the soft stones within with her tongue.

Her useless arms hanging limply behind her, over her arched back, the ponygirl lingered with the heavy pouch in her mouth. She felt honored that her master let her worship him so. She could feel her own sex moist with desire, her breasts, taut and heavy, her blood boiling within her. Drabik moaned and sighed as he absorbed the pleasure of her oral heat, the manipulation of his balls.

Almost reluctantly, after a prolonged and loving obeisance to the source of her trainer's precious spunk, the enraptured ponygirl abandoned her prize and returned her hot mouth to the rigid pole of flesh. She gripped it tightly between her lips and pressed down firmly as she slowly swallowed it, lowering her smooth, faceless, blue clad head until the fat knob on its tip breached her throat.

A hand laid itself lightly on her head and took hold of the long, straight, chestnut skein of hair that emerged from the top of her hood. It tightened around it and Lightning could feel her lover's hips shift beneath her as the hand took charge of her ministrations. She worked the shaft dutifully with her lips and tongue as her head was slowly brought up and down by the force of her trainer's grip. She could hear him moaning loudly as his need for completion grew. His cock thrust back up at her each time that the hand forced her head downwards.

Quicker now, with urgency, her master used her mouth and throat to assuage his frantic desire. Her breasts swayed and jumped beneath her, her bound hands behind her tightened into little fists. Again and again the rigid pole of flesh filled her, pushed down her throat and withdrew until her lips were just under the throbbing head. She heard her master groan, felt his body shudder and the wand inside her mouth began to pulse and jerk.

"Arrrrgh!" Drabik yelled as he began to pump a stream of his viscous, white fluid into her. His thighs shook, his hips pushed up at her. Delirious with joy at the product of her adorations, Lightning received each spurt of cum as if a gift from a god.

The sated ponygirl trainer let his cock soften in the pony's mouth, resting his hand on her blue clad head. Lightning waited for his signal to let the drooping flesh free from her lips and followed the lead of his hand as he drew her up to him. The taste of his spunk was redolent in her mouth as he rubbed his fingers over her lips. His other hand had taken possession of her harsh, leather gag and he presented it to her mouth. Regretfully, but obediently, Lightning parted her lips and let the hated, thick wad of leather enter. When her mouth was sealed, he locked it back behind her head. A tear formed in the pony's eye, unseen behind her Neoprene hood. She expected him to leave her now, to bind her either back to the rail that crossed her tiny stall, or to chain her to the floor on her pallet for the night. But the strong arm of the ponygirl trainer drew her to him and she nestled herself happily in the crux of his shoulder. Soon, she felt the even flow of his breath in his chest as he let somnia overtake him. She pressed her flesh softly against his and soon dozed off as well.

It was some hours later that she felt the masculine body beneath her stir. Drabik eased her off of him and then brought her to her feet. He led her to the small commode and pressed on her shoulders until she was positioned to release the contents of her bladder within it. She was grateful for the release, but reminded starkly of her bestial status. She did not know how many men she had performed this bodily function before. Maybe dozens. Each time, her lowly state was driven back home to her. Even a whore could pee in private. Even a slave girl could wipe her own wastes clean when done.

When she was finished, the master took a tissue and tenderly removed the tiny drops of fluids that had flowed over her naked, hairless cunt. He dropped it in the small basket next to the commode and drew her back to her feet. The lights of the ponygirl barn were turned down low and Lightning felt that her movements were almost dreamlike. Drabik let her to her pallet, which he had rolled out while she pissed, and laid her down on it on her back. Lightning, knowing that this was the last time that she would feel her lover's hands on her for many weeks, whined lowly behind her gag. He removed her heavy, black boots, baring her feet and then she felt him buckle her ankles together and affix them to a ring on the floor. Another chain connected her collar to rings on either side of her. A belt went around her thighs, shutting closed her still leaking, sticky, cum covered labial lips. She looked up through her tiny eyes holes and saw the darkened form of her master above her. His hand caressed her covered face one last time and he drew closed the Velcro tabs above her eyelets, sealing her into darkness.

Lightning listened as her master and lover dressed. There was the soft sound of fabric gliding across flesh, the stamp of boots on the floor as feet seated themselves within them. She sensed the man pausing, taking in the form of her naked breasts, belly and thighs. She imagined what he saw, her formless face, the bright blue letters of her name emblazoned across her upper chest, the stark yellow tattoo of the fierce wolf, the symbol of her indenture, on her belly, the tip of her hairless slit that was now squeezed between her muscular thighs. She mewed and writhed slightly in her bonds, all that the tight fittings allowed her. She could feel her large, soft breasts sway on her chest, the burning eyes of her master upon her. Then, the boots moved, the door to her stall swung open. And then it closed. She listened carefully as she heard the sound of his footsteps recede until there was only quiet.

Even at night, the pony barn was not absolutely silent. Once Drabik's firm, hard tread on the hardwood floor had disappeared, the background noises of the large structure rose up. Upwards of twenty five, naked, supine and bound ponies lay on their backs in the dimly lit building, in various stages of sleep. There was the sounds of light snoring, an occasional rattle of chains as a ponygirl tried to adjust herself in her sleep. Not far from where she lay, Lightning could hear the muffled sobs of a lonely, frightened ponygirl. The steady, measured steps of the night watchman echoed through the barn, at first faintly, and then louder as he passed by her stall.

A wave of misery flowed through the former Maddy Burnham as the reality of what awaited her the next day sunk home. The diminutive demon who was her driver no doubt had a painful, exquisite torture prepared for her. And then there would be the relentless, merciless training under his whip. She would not feel a tender touch for many weeks. Even the skinny, morose, black haired slave girl that assisted him would treat her roughly and callously, doling out punishments when her driver was not in the mood to mete them out himself.

Maddy had not cried for a long time. The fear which had seized her brought back to her the gross injustice of her horrible fate. What had she become? Not more than an hour or two ago she had experienced one of the greatest moments of joy that she had ever felt. And yet, as she lay here now, she saw it only as a measure of how far her nature had been corrupted. The man who had beaten her, tormented her, stolen her humanity had discharged into her mouth and she had felt, not horror, not revulsion, but joy!

The forlorn creature that had once been a vibrant, strong willed, self determined woman was now an animal so servile, so obsequious that she took delight in giving pleasure to the very man who had defiled her. And tomorrow. No, not tomorrow, since she sensed that the dawn was not too far away, today, she would be handed over to the cruelest, vilest man she had ever known. She would be his prisoner for weeks and weeks. And she would take pleasure, she knew that she would, in the crowds that would cheer her on, the challenge of the racing track, the thrill of victory.

Somewhere in the pony barn Maddy heard the sounds of a man's lust being visited upon one of her fellow creatures. His groaning and panting echoed through the warren of wooden stalls. Fainter, but still audible, was the whines of pleasure of the assaulted ponygirl in heat, reveling in her ravishment, just as she had done just hours before. She rubbed her naked thighs together almost unconsciously. Was she so corrupted that the mere sounds of coitus were enough to make her pussy burn? She was. And she hated herself for it.

The unhappy former human female clamped her blinded eyes shut and took her mind back to the mental safe harbor that she had created for herself. The past was gone. She was what she was. If it was her fate to be a ponygirl, then she must accept it. And as a ponygirl, she was a mere instrument for her masters. Long ago, she had determined that if she was condemned to a life of servitude, if she was recreated in the form of a beast, that she would be the best one that she could ever be. The girl Maddy was dead. She was Lightning now. She would endure the travails imposed upon her by her viciously cruel driver. She would endure the training, the humiliations, the silent, non-volitional life imposed upon her. But she would run and run and run. She would beat them all. She was a ponygirl champion and she would be again. She swore it to herself.

* * * * * * * * * * * * * * * *

Somehow, finally, sleep overtook the prostrate creature. She awoke with a start when she heard the door to her ponygirl stall swing open and close again. Hands released her thighs, ankles and collar and she was pulled to her feet. Hands guided her to her small commode and she released the liquids that she had stored overnight. Her eyelets were still closed and she did not know which of the many men who serviced the ponies had come for her. She felt her pussy wiped roughly by the man and she was pushed down to her knees and turned to face the wall. She heard behind her the sounds of a bowl being filled with water and the familiar sound of a brush swishing in the bowl, drawing up a fine, thick lather. Her shield gag was unbuckled and unknown hands unclipped her tight fitting, Neoprene hood from her collar drawing it up over her head.

The bright light of the morning caused Lightning's eyes to squint and blink as a soft brush applied the soapy lather to her head. She had endured this ritual many times. While a strong, rough hand held her neck and chin in a vice-like grip, a razor stroked gently over her scalp, eliminating the fine growth that had developed there over the last twenty four hours. The ritual served as a daily reminder to her that her body was not hers to control. Ironically, she had come to appreciate the daily removal of the evidence of her humanity. She wanted nothing to remind her of the past, not even the growth of a minute stubble. When the man was done, he would rub a cool lotion over her naked head and face then reinstall her hood, a new one, clean for the day's work and toil, and reinstall her gag.

During this momentary unveiling of her facial features, her face was always pointed away from the groom who was servicing her. No one was to see her face. Oddly enough, she had become happy that she could hide her face away, that her former humanity was hidden, buried. If one of the men had looked into her face now, she would cringe with humiliation. It was the only part of her that was private. It was the only way that she could maintain her small, last vestige of herself.

Once she was rehooded and regagged, the man turned her again and pushed her back against the wall of her stall. Automatically, she lifted her knees and spread her legs, presenting her naked loins to him. Through her small eyelets, which were now open, she recognized the heavyset, blond haired young man who was servicing her this morning. He had serviced her many times. She did not know his name, didn't know any of their names. But she could not recall him ever mistreating her. He wore thick, brown workpants and a copper colored long sleeved shirt open down to the third button to reveal a well developed chest. His blond hair reached to his shoulders and his face was hairless. In a workmanlike manner, he applied the lather to her loins and then proceeded to shave away the tiny follicles that had erupted there.

Lightning's pussy began to glisten with incipient arousal at the man's practiced handling of her sex and lower belly, for she knew that very soon this man would bring her to arousal and climax. It was part of the daily routine. The only thing that varied was whether her morning groom would use his hands, his mouth, or his rigid prick to drive her passions. Her nipples were already stiffened in anticipation when he took a wet cloth and washed the remnants of the lather away from her clean shaven mons.

The man put away the shaving utensils and turned back to the expectant ponygirl. He smiled at her and ran his hands down the length of the insides of her pale, firm, widespread thighs. He pressed her hairless labial lips together gently and rubbed them against each other, squeezing out the moist evidence of her arousal. His hands passed over her hips and caressed her stomach, covering up momentarily the bright yellow, angry wolf emblazoned there. He seized her engorging breasts and caressed them softly until he elicited a quiet moan from her.

The man was apparently deciding how he would administer her orgasm to her. He pulled gently on her stiffened teats, lifting her heavy breasts from her chest. Her lusts rising, Lightning shifted her hips and gripped the thick wad of leather in her mouth tightly with her teeth.

As if finally inspired, the young, blond headed man took hold of the ring that protruded from her septum and pulled the ponygirl forward. Lightning hated the thick ring that dangled from her nose and any use of it caused a flood of shame to well up inside her. But it was there to be used, not as mere decoration.

Lightning followed the lead of her nose until she was kneeling in the center of her stall. The groom clipped the nose ring to an iron ring in the floor, forcing the pony's torso down. He maneuvered himself behind her and placed his heavy hands on her haunches, caressing the firm, pale globes. He passed a hand down between her outstretched thighs and stroked the moistened slit between them until his fingers slid easily in and out of her burning crevasse. Lightning heard the sound of his zipper falling and, after a moment, felt the bulbous end of his cock press against the small, brown ring of her rear entrance.

Drabik, during Lightning's initial training, had broken the pony into the pleasures of ass fucking. For two weeks, he had covered her sex with a steel mesh so that she could not be penetrated there and had locked her gag onto her so that anyone who wanted to use her would have to use the smaller, tighter entrance of her rear. Finally, after the frustrated pony had learned to orgasm through the use of this aperture alone, he had released her. Now it was if she had developed a second cunt and the rasping of a thick, hot cock along the tender lips of her anus drove her easily to ecstasy.

So although her pussy burned with need, Lightning was not unhappy that the man had chosen to use her this way. She sighed as the engorged meat pushed easily past the still smaller entry. Lightning had learned how to soften her muscles there to facilitate her masters' desires. She moaned as she felt her bowels fill until the back of the man's thighs pressed against her rear. She moaned again as he began his motion, slowly drawing back until just the head of his steely cock rested within her and then pressed forward again, delivering a wave of almost unbearable pleasure through her.

Lightning could not and had no reason to hide her passion. She rocked back and forth to encourage the man's movements, whined and moaned as she felt her lusts building higher and higher. The golden brass ring tugged at her nose as she lost herself in her excitement. Her anxious cries of pleasure overcame the thick wad of leather in her mouth. When she heard the man groan his own pleasure, her release was triggered and wave after wave of intolerable excitement flowed through her. Her empty pussy throbbed and contracted, her breasts ached with their fullness. And when she felt the throbbing of the man's cock, the tightening of the man's grasp upon her hips, felt him pound his sturdy thighs hard against her firm rear globes, she came again, screeching and biting down on the thick leather within her mouth.

The man lay against her as he recovered his senses. Her heart was pounding in her chest from her exertions, her breath, deep and labored. After a brief recovery, she felt his softening meat slip from within her and heard him step back to the faucet and wash his piece of her wastes. He left her there for a few minutes, kneeling with her nose ring still affixed to the floor, her breasts crushed against her thighs, her body still tingling, her mind reliving her moments of ecstasy. When he returned, he brought with him her morning porridge.

Lightning was left alone while she slurped down her morning repast. Although her gag was removed and she was alone, she did not even think of trying to use her long stilled voice. She had seen a pony suffer a dreadful punishment for speaking once and she never wanted to add to her misfortunes in that way. Besides, who would she speak to? She didn't even know if any of the other ponies spoke English. What would she say to them? Help?

When the groom returned, Lightning knew that the time had come for her to get ready to be conveyed to her driver. It was with great trepidation that she suffered the cleaning of her mouth by the groom, the reinstallation of her gag. The last thing was her readornment with her heavy black ponygirl boots. The groom rubbed a lotion onto her valuable feet and then reimprisoned them, tying the laces tight. He brought her to her full height by pulling up on the ring to her collar, connected a leash to her nose ring and led her from her stall.

Lightning remembered well the path that led past the huge mansion belonging to her owner over a small set of hills and down to the large area which served as the ponygirl park. Her groom led her by her leashed nose along the black macadam pathway wordlessly. No one talked to a ponygirl and so it was not unusual that the man who had groomed and fucked her a short while ago did not relate to her where they were going. But Lightning knew.

As they crested the hills, about three hundred yards away from the mansion, Maddy saw the array of ponygirl wagons sprawled along the copse of trees. Other ponygirls were being led there both ahead and behind her, almost like some kind of strange parade. Each blue headed, naked former female was led by a single rough looking groom and delivered to the campsite of her driver for the season. Jerzi's campsite was out on the far edge of the scattered trailers and Lightning experienced the bustle and confusion of the first day of racing training on the estate. Some of the other ponies had been delivered earlier and one or two carts passed along the dirt trails that were interspersed throughout the pony park. These were not the battered and worn carts and carriages used for regular training. These were the shiny, splendidly outfitted machines used during the formal racing season. They all carried the blue and gold colors that represented Grobgy's racing teams. And the ponies who had been hitched to their carts already wore, not the dark blue Neoprene hoods that were their standard adornment, but hoods with hemispheres of blue and gold, their racing caps.

Pretty little naked slave girls hustled to and fro around the camp. They were the property of the drivers, specially trained to service the racing animals. Lightning noted the wide variety of heraldic tattoos on their bellies through her tiny eye slits as they passed on the trail. Most of them wore leather shield gags over their mouths and chins, enforcing strictly the general rule of silence for slaves. But yet Lightning couldn't help but envy them their relative freedom, virtually liberty as it compared with the life that she led. Their hands were free, their head bore their free manes of hair. Although they wore collars and leather bracelets around their ankles and wrists, they were unfettered. And they had faces. They were still recognizable as persons. And she and her sister ponies were not.

Lightning's stomach grew queasy as she approached her driver's campsite. She saw first the shiny, gold plated sulky cart parked next to her driver's trailer. She whined in fear as she was led towards it. The wooden seat and the frame of the wheels were of highly polished wood. A blue and gold pennant fluttered from the rear. When they entered the camp, Jerzi, Lightning's master and God for the next two months, was nowhere to be seen. Kneeling patiently in the middle of the small grassy center of the camp was Jerzi's slave girl. She was as skinny and scrawny as Lightning remembered her, with stringy, shoulder length black hair and drawn, almost gaunt features. She was wearing one of the leather shield gags and she rose as Lightning was led into the small paddock. With a flash of her harsh, narrow eyes, she took the lead from the groom and led Lightning over to a post that had been pounded into the ground.

Lightning stood there, her nose ring hitched by a short chain to the post, for a long time. The slave girl had made a cursory examination of her, feeling her thighs and running her hands over her belly. She pinched Lightning's nipples harshly and then turned her around to let her hands wander over her pale rear globes. The pony acquiesced in her maltreatment, knowing that she had no right to object or resist. And anyway, she knew that much worst was soon to come. But the callousness with which the little slave girl handled her naked body made her stomach roil with unhappiness.

The slave girl then returned to the center of the paddock and knelt, her naked thighs spread wide, her hands resting behind her, awaiting the arrival of her master.

When Lightning turned around, she saw that the groom was gone. Her last contact with the relative safety of the pony barn had disappeared. What she had been dreading had now happened and she was doomed to do nothing more than stand and await the presence of the man who she feared more than any other.

There was enough lead on the leash that bound Lightning to the pole to let her circle around it. She wanted to kneel and give ease to her trembling legs, but the leash was not long enough. Her palms were sweaty with fear and her heart pumped madly in her chest. It was difficult to see well through her tiny eye holes and she tilted and bent her blue clad head back and forth, an animalistic gesture that made her appear just like the pony that she was, to watch as people came and went along the dirt track, fearing that each one she saw would be the man whose presence she awaited.

Finally she recognized the diminutive stature of her driver. He was wearing tiny little denim pants and a light green t-shirt which pulled tightly over his well muscled chest. The dwarf had scruffy, black hair that flowed over his ears and a short, dark, black beard that covered his face. In his hand was a four foot long, leather encased whip. His features were large and his head appeared oversized for his little body. He was a grotesque simulacrum of a man, but his distorted dimensions and hoary outlook gave him a dreadful dark beauty. His movements were sure and almost arrogant, his demeanor of a man of strength and determination. He was precisely as Lightning remembered him.

The small man strode purposefully into the little enclosure. Each individual camp site was bordered by six foot high, long, blue and gold silken panels, set onto stakes so that each driver's territory was well demarked. The panels, which afforded the campsite a modicum of privacy, fluttered in the light breeze as if announcing some gay holiday. The dwarf glanced up quickly at the distraught ponygirl and then issued a sharp command to his kneeling minion, emphasized by a sharp crack of the whip that he held in his hand. The lash struck the slave girl across her side, curling around to her back and she gave a little shriek behind her leather gag. She hopped up immediately and rushed into the small camper that served as the ponygirl driver's home in the camp. A moment later, she reemerged with a bottle of vodka and a small glass. She handed them to Jerzi, bowing slightly as she did so and then resumed her kneeling position.

Jerzi took his bottle and glass and sat in a custom made, cloth, colored folding chair. The chair had a little table next to it and, after pouring himself a tumbler full of vodka, he placed the clear, shiny bottle down on top of it. He stared down at the transparent liquid in his glass for a moment, as if considering some issue of great portent, and then poured the contents back into his throat. His dark eyes winced as the fiery liquid slid down his esophagus. He poured himself another glass and then leaned back in his chair.

The small man's will dominated the small enclosure as if he were a tiny demon, able to cast an evil spell over all that he surveyed. To Lightning, the silence of the little encampment was stifling. She could hear the background noises of the activity elsewhere in the camp, but the shouted commands, the trundle of carriage wheels, the clanging of pots and pans, the occasional crack of a whip, all just served to heighten the tense quietude of the grassy paddock. The little man just sat there, his brooding eyes seeing into some other world. Lightning's fear gripped her like a fever. She paced nervously around her pole, first one way, then the other, a whimper escaping from behind her gag randomly. She almost wished that she were lashed securely to the pole instead of being given enough of a lead to take one or two steps away. If she were held motionless, she would be able to lose herself in her confinements, let the tightness and security of her bonds overwhelm her mind. But her relative freedom let all her anxiety manifest itself, and she paced back and forth almost unconsciously around the pole like a worried, caged, circus animal.

The dwarf took his time in sipping down his second drink. It was a beautiful day, almost cloudless and the faint hints of fall that had been in the air the last few days had been extinguished. Part of him was still angry about Grobgy's decision to have Lightning run the 3000 meter, and he gripped his glass tightly when his morose thoughts turned to it. He wanted to go head to head with his brother Giorgi, who would be driving the brown colored pony this season in the 1500. They would not have met in the regular season anyway. Grobgy's estate was in the southern tier of the national sport and they would run most of their meets against the estates south of the Balinkas River. Burnham's estate was in the north and, except for an occasional interdivisional meet scheduled to even out the competition, would be matched against estates up there.

But, Jerzi had been dreaming of a head to head match against his brother in the championship tournament for weeks. And then there was the fact that Lightning would have been a near shoo-in for the 1500 meter championship this fall. There were few ponies who had championed in two tournaments in the same year and fewer drivers, at least on the same ponies. The sport had been revived ten years ago and there had been only fifteen tournaments, the first few years having only one tournament a year. There was a huge cash prize to the driver of a championship pony and great prestige. Now he had to drive Lightning in a new division, race against ponies she had not seen yet, prove herself all over again.

When his bile had grown strong enough, the small, angry ponygirl driver barked a command to his slave girl who jumped immediately to her feet as if she had been poised for the sound of his gravelly voice. In fact, she had, knowing that hesitancy in meeting the desires of her cruel master could mean excruciating punishment. Natasha, once a petit, pretty, lighthearted waitress in a small town lodged in the Carpathian region of Romania, had been a slave girl for over five years. She had served the demonic dwarf for three. At the time she first met him, she had been an inmate in a small, sophisticated, first class whorehouse in the capital, Dlitski. She had been allowed to wear pretty, fashionable, revealing, little dresses as she preened and displayed herself for customers. But one night, this little man had come in. He had selected her and she had spent a night of torment with him. In the morning, to her dismay, she had been gagged and hooded and led away.

Natasha scurried around the little paddock in response to her owner's command. She took a stool and, standing on it, swung a steel arm away from the side of the camper. She opened a large trunk that sat outside next to the ponygirl cage and withdrew a leather harness from it. She ran over to the ponygirl and, placing the stool next to her, stepped up on it.

Natasha was only 5'2" tall, almost a full foot taller than her diminutive master, but Lightning was closer to 5'10". And with her boots on, she was even taller. Natasha needed the additional height to run a broad leather strap from the harness under the pony's locked arms and across her chest above her bountiful breasts. The strap was fastened closed with a heavy buckle, and Natasha drew it tight so that it lay just beneath the pony's collar. Additional straps went over the shoulders and around her waist. When these were fastened, she leaned over and freed the pony's leash from the pole and led her over to where the heavy, metal bar extended from the side of the camper.

Climbing up again on the stool, Natasha linked a chain that hung down from the bar to a hook in the middle of the strap behind Lightning's back. Pulling on the other end of the chain, leaning on it with all her weight, Natasha was able to force the ponygirl to her tippy toes, the strap behind her back pulling her upwards. She fastened the chain and then stepped away from the clearly distraught creature. Her mission complete, she returned the stool to its prior location and then resumed her kneeling, submissive pose.

Lightning obeyed the pulls and tugs of the slave girl without hesitation, albeit reluctantly. She could see the dwarf looking at her with disdainful, malicious eyes. The whip he had brought with him was lying at his feet and she knew that in a moment, he would get up and begin to deliver the torment that she had so long dreaded. Sweat ran down her shapely, pale, fine tuned body. Her mouth was dry and her throat constricted. And she had to pee.

Knowing ponygirls well and what fear did to them, Jerzi ordered his slave girl to service the unhappy pony. Ponies learned quickly the punishment for pissing willy nilly in the paddock that served as their home during the racing season. Ordinarily, on the racing track, or elsewhere that their endeavors took them, they peed where and when they felt the urge, bending their knees slightly, spreading their legs and letting the golden stream flow between their black boots. But peeing in the paddock would ultimately bring about an undesirable odiferous atmosphere and so it was forbidden. Like dogs that had learned to sniff and scratch at a door when the need to eliminate arose in them, ponygirls learned to make a little gesture with their hips, bending their knees and spreading their thighs in solicitude. An alert trainer or his slave girl would accommodate them, if it was convenient. Otherwise they would have to suffer their full bladders until they were serviced.

Natasha went over to the trunk and pulled out a narrow, gleaming steel bedpan and a small rag. She brought the pan to Lightning and nudged it between her thighs until her hairless labial lips were above it. Lightning gratefully widened her thighs as much as she could, her efforts encumbered by the chain lifting her onto her toes, and released a stream of hot fluid into the pan. When she was done, the pan was removed, the rag dragged across her naked pussy. Natasha spilled the pan's contents into a jar by the trunk kept there for that purpose and wiped the pan with the rag. They were tossed back into the trunk. Once a week, a truck came along the camp and the large jar was emptied.

Although shamed at her need for the girl's assistance in performing this private bodily function, and relieved of her immediate distress, Lightning's mind soon returned to her foreboding over the torment she knew that she was about to suffer. She flinched when she saw the dwarf get up from his chair and lean over and pick up the long, thin whip.

Wordlessly, the small man approached the target of his wrath. While other ponygirl drivers tended to coddle and nurture their temporary charges, Jerzi and his brother Giorgi believed that fear of pain was the greatest motivator when it came to ponygirls. This had to be established right from the start. Win or suffer. That was the only thing that the ponygirls needed to know. Jerzi wanted to squeeze every ounce of strength and endurance out of his ponies and, he knew in his heart, this was the best way to do it. Occasionally, a pony would ride itself right into the ground rather than disappoint him. But that was just one of the hazards that a driver ran when he drove a ponygirl or a ponygirl team. And a good driver, except in the very most important races, would be able to feel and see when a ponygirl had given her all, was washed out.

Jerzi could not see the tense, fearful face of his victim, covered as it was by the tight fitting blue hood. Her features were almost nonexistent. Only the bump of the nose gave away the fact that there was a former human female under there, even the eyes were hidden away. And her mouth was covered by the leather shield that was attached to the thick gag in her mouth and so he could not see her tight, trembling lips. But he could see the sheen of sweat that covered her. He could see the plump, inviting, naked breasts shivering as they echoed the fear induced shudders that wracked the ponygirl's body. He could see the rock hard nipples, evidence, not of the pony's arousal, but of her fear.

He walked around the pony slowly, rubbing his hard, calloused hands over her flesh, taking his ownership of the tall, desirable former human female. He felt her thighs knowingly, measuring their strength and toning. He stepped in front of her and, raising his short arms, hefted her draping, billowing breasts in his hands appreciatively, running his thumbs over the taut nipples. He nudged her thighs apart and captured the hairless mons in his gnarly hand, pressing the delicate lips together until Lightning moaned in discomfort. He then stroked the tender lips until they obediently began to engorge. When the narrow slit between them began to glisten with the pony's unwilling, automatic arousal, he traced the opening with his thick finger and teased the little bud at the top.

She was fine specimen of an animal, Jerzi knew that. And she was in fine shape, ready to run, ready for the intense, remorseless additional training she would undergo in the next two weeks. Well, almost ready. There was one thing that needed to be done first.

The powerful, tiny man, after leaning over to connect the rings on the pony's two boots together, stepped back from the ponygirl and positioned himself slightly to the side. He reared his hand back, the hand holding the long, leather covered whip, and let fly. A loud 'crack!' emerged from where the leather struck the tender skin of the pony's belly. Her whole body jumped and a long, fretful whine emerged from her gag. A thin line of red arose from her flesh, just along the bottom of the bright yellow wolfen tattoo.

Lightning felt the fire leap across her upper loins. What she had feared was now coming to pass. She had promised herself that she would hold her demeanor in check, that she would resist the urge to moan and cry, to dance and struggle, to wail and beg for surcease, but that all left her now. She hated to be whipped, avoided it at all costs, despised herself for her inability to withstand the pain and humiliation of being the object of a master's recriminations and/or cruel pleasure. For some of the masters beat ponies just for the fun of it. As long as it did not impede the pony's functionality, no one really cared.

Her whole body trembling and shaking as she anticipated the second blow, Lightning watched as the demonic driver circled behind her. She could not turn to see him. Suddenly, simultaneously, she heard the tell tale hiss of the whip as it was brought swiftly forward and then a burning laceration across her buttocks. She howled into her gag with pain.

The blows came now with swiftness and regularity. Across the back of her joined thighs, across the front, across her breasts, her belly and back again. Lightning's body was like a burning plinth, dancing and jumping as she reacted to each frightful, intense kiss of the lash. She clenched her hidden eyes fiercely tight and bit down desperately on her leather gag in a fruitless attempt to stifle her screams and muffled entreaties for relief. It was the only time that she ever tried to speak, when she was being belabored cruelly by a whip. But the syllables she screamed out desperately were not really words, not volitional, not intended to actually communicate anything. They were just sounds that her body made out of almost ancient habit.

Jerzi's small body was covered with sweat when he finished. The pony's body was criss-crossed with red lines. Her shins, her breasts, her thighs, her belly. Even her arms and hands had been whipped, the top of her back in the space not covered by the long, wide leather belt that hung from the back of her collar and captured her useless arms and wrists. The pony's chest heaved as she struggled to contain her bitter, wrenching sobs. Her hood was drenched from her tears and her nose was running wildly. Jerzi waited for the pony to recover a modicum of control over herself. He then signaled his slave girl to release the pony from the chain that held her in place.

Lightning sank to her knees when she was released. Her eyes were now almost level with those of her tormentor's. She could see the hard, callous determination there. The message had been conveyed. She would do anything and all that he wanted with all of the energy in her body. He was her master, her lord.

Jerzi tossed the whip aside and reached forward to the ponygirl's collar. She felt him fumbling at her neck and then saw, as his hands withdrew, that he had removed from there the golden medallion that she wore that symbolized and announced her status as a ponygirl champion.

Lightning groaned with unhappiness when she saw the emblem in her master's hands. It was hers, she had earned it and she wore it with pride. If she had to be a ponygirl, she wanted to be the best, to stand out, to feel just one iota better than the other poor, hooded, naked former women that surrounded her. And now he had taken it from her.

She watched unhappily as she saw him place the golden disk in his pocket. The message was clear. She could not rest on her laurels. That was then and this was now. She would have to earn her medal all over again. Deep inside her, she knew that he master was right. She could not coast to victory. And the cruelty, the pain, the hard treatment she would and had just received, she knew that was what she really needed. It would make her fast. Hard and fast. And she would win. She would earn her medal back, or she would die trying.

There was one more humiliation in store for the abased ponygirl. Jerzi reached behind her head and unbuckled her gag, tossing it to the ground. He pulled his large, rigid cock from his pants and presented it to her mouth. While Jerzi was diminutive in stature, there was nothing small or child like about his cock and it stood as thick and tall as any man's.

Lightning bent over, her large breasts touching her knees, and opened her mouth to receive her lord's manhood. His hand took hold of her ponytail behind her head and he slipped the hot, hard meat over her tongue and deep into her mouth.

Normally, Lightning would have closed her lips over the tantalizing meat, covered it with strokes of her skilled tongue, sucked on it gently to urge her possessor to pleasure. But this was not her driver's desire; she had learned that many months ago the hard way. He did not seek her caresses. He only sought her use. For the next many weeks, Lightning would be deprived of the sexual completions that she had been taught to desire and need. Until and unless she had pleased her master, at the end of a successful race, she would not feel the hot throbbing spasms of her master's cock. She would not experience the delightful and redeeming contractions of her cunt in pleasure. She would be used as a forlorn receptacle for her driver's desires and his spunk.

The thick, hard meat found the back of Lightning's throat and pierced it. Lightning coughed slightly as she accommodated the rigid pole. She felt the driver's manhood slowly stroke back and forth in her mouth, each time seeking the constrictiveness of her throat. She gagged and sputtered as he ruthlessly violated her. And then the hand tightened on her ponytail. The thighs of the little man quivered. He quickly pulled his tool from Lightning's mouth and grabbed it with his free hand. Keeping it poised at the entrance of he pony's still open mouth, he jerked and tugged at it until it began to pulse and spasm. He closed his eyes and leaned back as his spunk jumped from his cock's tip and into the awaiting, submissive mouth of the ponygirl. She could feel it spurting onto her dormant tongue. The familiar acrid, salty taste flooded her mouth. She dared not swallow. She would have to show it to him when he was done.

The dwarf groaned as he shot his last spurt of cum into the awaiting mouth of the blue headed ponygirl. He took a moment to relish the aftermath of his orgasm. Lightning held her mouth open so that he could see the product of his loins there. He nodded to her, giving her permission to swallow and then barked an order to his slave girl who had knelt watching the torment and use of the ponygirl dispassionately. Or not quite dispassionately. Three years of almost incessant cruelty and abuse had twisted Natasha's soul and she took delight in the torture of the tall, strong ponygirl. Over the next weeks, she would take whatever opportunity she could to add to the dismal treatment of the pony. Something in Natasha yearned for someone or something to be lower than she was, more abject, more helpless. It delighted her to see the big, strong ponygirl suffer. If it were not for the ponygirls, she might still be back in the relative comfort of that whorehouse where her master had found her. She wouldn't have to bear the displeasure and cruelty of the driver when the ponygirl didn't please him, or his punishment when she did not service the ponygirl just right. And she begrudged the ponygirl's use of her master's cock, whether he came in her or not. It was the only pleasure in her life to have him plow her orifices. And when he was using the ponygirl, he wasn't using her.

Jerzi went into the camper while Natasha dragged the ponygirl over to the side of the encampment by her ponygirl cage. Later, Lightning would spend many hours ensconced in the tiny steel prison, usually hidden away from the world, covered by the thick, black tarp that sat over it now.

Natasha reached into the trunk and pulled out Lightning's racing harness. She unbuckled the punishment harness and quickly applied the racing harness to her body. It contained rings along its side and back for the attachment of the leads to the sulky she would pull and on her hips where the polished wooden poles that led from the sides of the cart would be affixed to her hips. While Lightning knelt forlornly in the grass, she ran back to the trailer and emerged with one of the blue and gold hoods that Lightning would wear day and night until the racing season was over. Being careful not to expose her naked face to any passers by, Natasha removed the pony's dark blue Neoprene hood and recovered her face and head with the blue and gold one, pulling the long, chestnut ponytail through the hole in the top. When the new multicolored hood was affixed to the faceless ponygirl's collar, Natasha inserted into Lightning's mouth the leather covered, steel bit that she wore when pulling a cart. It had a steel pate that depressed her tongue cruelly. When the leads that would be attached to either side were pulled, the pony's head would have to respond instantly or she would suffer excruciating pain. The cruel instrument left the pony's lips exposed and stretched into a strange grimace.

After she was properly outfitted, Lightning was brought to the racing sulky. Natasha had her back in between the wooden poles and kneel while she fastened the long leather traces to her harness and her bit and then attached the poles to her hips. When done, she made her stand and, leading her forwards with her finger curled around the golden ring in her nose, positioned the pony and the cart by the entranceway to the campsite.

At this point, Jerzi emerged from the camper. He had redressed himself in the racing colors of the estate, silken shirt and pants striped blue and gold. He wore a cap divided equally in the two colors, matching the hood that Lightning now wore. Without hesitation or comment, he leapt atop the seat to the small, lightweight sulky cart. Lightning could feel the cart depress from his weight through the poles on her hips. There was the crack of a whip which landed expertly, not too hard, but fierce enough to lend encouragement, on her right rear cheek. "*Avant, Molnya!*" the rough voice of the expert ponygirl driver called and Lightning sprang into life. As she felt the weight of the cart on her shoulders and sides and stepped into the dirt lane outside the camp, she broke into a trot.

CHAPTER FOUR
PLANS FOR THE FUTURE

The former Chicago whore known as Jackie, now known as Chocolate, was on her fifth lap of the finely groomed, wide, racing track of the Burnham estate. Her legs were tired, her chest was heaving, and her ass was sore from the bite of the riding whip carried by her determined and callous Russian driver. After her warm up, this was her third set of five laps this morning. Her driver was pushing her hard, harder than she was used to. She wanted to stop, wanted to slow down, but her experiences of the morning persuaded her to maintain the pace as well as she could.

Chocolate had had a similar experience to Lightning when she first met the strange looking dwarf who was her driver, Giorgi Gromyko, except, that for her, the vision of the tiny, demonic looking man who would be her driver had been quite startling. Foolishly, she had coughed out a little laugh as her lead was handed over to him, an expression she soon had many reasons to regret.

She had been surprised when she was led to the pony park on Burnham's estate. She had never raced before and no one had bothered to explain to her how things worked or that this morning her custody would be turned over to her driver for the fall racing season. She had thought it strange the unusual activity in the ponygirl barn the night before. Many of the grooms and trainers were getting their 'last licks', so to speak, with the ponies before they were sent away to the park. She, herself, had been a popular attraction due to her unusual skin color. There was no racial prejudice in the ponygirl barn, and the men had grown to appreciate her smooth, tawny brown skin, its delicate luster and her genuine enthusiasm when fucked.

Giorgi, Jerzi's brother, had beaten her severely on her arrival. Unlike Jerzi, Giorgi allowed himself to visit his lusts fully on the ponies in his charge and had plowed Chocolate vigorously fore and aft when he had finished adorning her body with bright, red stripes. In fact, Giorgi's theory on the subject was quite the opposite of Jerzi's. He believed in having total sexual control over his charges. Chocolate would spend the next twelve weeks or so in an almost steady state of sexual excitement. Only on racing day would her lusts be denied. On those days, all of her sexual frustration would be poured into her efforts at winning her heat.

But he had other means of enforcing terror on the defenseless ponygirl. He was versed in the use of long, sharp needles with which he sought out delicate nerves in the pony's body, driving her into exquisite pain. He used clamps and other pressure devices on her intimate parts. On days when he was especially dissatisfied, he would insert a large steel ball in the pony's mouth. By turning a screw on the end, sharp needles would emerge which he would elongate until the pony's mouth was fully extended. He would leave her standing in the middle of the small paddock outside his camper, bound to a stake, the points of the spikes digging deeper and deeper into her mouth. The next day, when the steel bit was mounted between her teeth, every little pull on it would send her into a paroxysm of agony. And he had some other tricks too.

His slave girl assistant was a blond haired Latvian girl. She was short of stature like Natasha, but rather than being a veritable wastrel like the black haired girl who served Jerzi, Ilona was a voluptuous, shapely female. She wore her thick, blond hair in a braid that descended to the middle of her back. While her owner could be cruel to her, her moans of pain could be heard sometimes late at night from inside his trailer as he mistreated her, he was generally indifferent to her as long as she did her job, pleased him when he demanded it and stayed beautiful.

Ilona didn't have the streak of meanness that had developed in Natasha either, and she treated Chocolate in a kindly, but stern, manner. She knew that Giorgi would frown on any sign of friendship towards the former human female, and so Ilona kept her emotional distance from the creature even though her heart often went out to the unfortunate former woman.

After beating and fucking her on her first day, Giorgi took the brown skinned ponygirl out to the racing track for training. Chocolate was dressed in a black and gold hood and harnessed to the shiny sulky cart. She was surprised at how light it was compared to the cart that she had been pulling. And she was virtually dumfounded when, trotting obediently out to the racing track she got her first view of the beautiful, well cared for track and the large, luxurious grandstand that stood beside it. Other teams were out training, hauling their finely decorated, well appointed carts and carriages over the soft, clean dirt. Chocolate, in her former life, one that she one day hoped to return to, had loved going to the track. Ironically, it was the trotters that she like to see and gamble on. There was something about their stylized pace, the whirring wheels of their carts, the stiff attentiveness of their drivers that had excited her. She had blown a lot of money there. And now, here she was, running like a pacer horse, her own little driver mounted behind her.

Chocolate didn't have much opportunity to enjoy the view of the modern style track and the gracious landscaping that surrounded it. First of all, she was limited in her sight by what she could see through the little holes in her hood. And secondly, her driver drove her fiercely along the track, cracking his whip on her rear. She quickly decided to pour all of her efforts into the task at hand rather than risk a renewal of his wrath.

Burnham had contracted for extensive renovations to the grand stand when he had assumed control and ownership of the estate and the workmen were still putting on the final touches. Small groups of them, idle in their work, stood around the rail watching the pretty, naked ponygirls strut their stuff. They were joined by various touts and aficionados of the sport trying to get a line on Burnham's stable. There was extensive interest in the brown skinned pony. Lightning had been the first yearling, a pony new to her bit, that had won a sulky championship. The scuttlebutt was that Chocolate was another comer and that she would place high in the season's rankings. The American billionaire was considered audacious to run her in the sulky and there were many who resented the foreign intrusion into their sport. But, when the boots hit the dirt and the starting flag was waved, it would be the fastest, best competitor who would win the race, and if Chocolate had the right stuff, the smart money would be on her.

Chocolate fully expected to get a breather after her fifth lap, but when she passed the finish pole, Giorgi gave her a sharp crack of the whip and she unhappily pushed on. They didn't stop at the sixth lap, nor the seventh or the eighth or ninth. By the tenth lap, Chocolate thought that she would die from exertion. Between each deep, painful breath, she was sobbing. Her driver was relentless, his whip working her back and rear raw. Finally, the brown skinned pony could run no more. She stumbled, something she hadn't done since her first days of training, and then she fell. The traces stopped her from falling prostrate on the ground, but her knees plunged into the soft dirt of the track, the cruel bit in her mouth pulled tight, her shoulders were wrenched back.

In a flash, Giorgi hopped off of the stilled cart. He carried in his small right hand a thick wooden dowel. Standing in front of the breathless, miserable pony until he was sure that he had her attention, he smashed the two foot long dowel first into her right upper arm and then her left. The dowel landed with a sickening 'thump!' as it bruised the lax, disused muscles. Chocolate groaned in agony. She lifted her head as if to plead for mercy and saw the fierce determination in her driver's eyes. Three men who had been standing idly by the guardrail laughed among themselves. Chocolate's stock had just gone done quite considerably. But Giorgi didn't care about that. Betting on ponygirl races was verboten for the drivers, a rule that was enforced with the muzzle of a low caliber pistol.

The angry dwarf, dressed in the silken black and gold colors of the estate, gave Chocolate a gruff, one word order in his raspy voice. When Chocolate hesitated, he struck her again twice, once in each arm. Chocolate howled at the pain and rushed herself to her feet. Giorgi hopped back on the cart and snapped the reigns signaling a fast start.

Groaning her self pity and dismay, Chocolate sprung back into life.

Giorgi forced the pony to run one more lap at full speed and then reined the miserable, exhausted ponygirl to a halt. He let her pause for about thirty seconds and then signaled her to begin her cool down laps.

It was an exhausted, dismally unhappy pony that pulled the sulky cart into Giorgi's encampment. Ilona had been waiting patiently, kneeling in the center, her leather gag installed in her mouth. When the pony entered the grassy area, Giorgi jumped off of the seat and strode purposely over to the small camper that was his home. He stepped in and slammed the door shut.

The pretty blond slave girl unhooked Chocolate from her traces and brought her over to the side of the camper. A shower hookup was there and she placed the lethargic, docile pony underneath it. She turned it on and a cool spray of water rained down on the ponygirl.

Ilona had known what to expect on the return of her master. She had seen it before. She felt sorry for the pony and tenderly rubbed a soft, soapy sponge all over her sweaty body. Dark bruises had already arisen on the pony's arms and she patted the areas softly, not wanting to cause the animal any additional pain. When the shower was over, she dried her off with a large, soft towel and released the steel bit from between her teeth. She took a large bottle of cold water and let the pony drink.

Chocolate had welcomed the warm water running down all over her punished body. In the places where her morning, welcoming beating from her driver had lacerated her skin, she experienced momentary stabs of pain as the water and soap ran into them. The cold water that the slave girl gave her to drink was refreshing and very welcome. She looked at the business like face of the pretty girl and decided that it would be a grave error to express her thanks and so she remained silent while the girl retrieved the leather gag that served as her silencer and pushed it back into her mouth. When it was tightly locked behind her head, the girl led her over to a large, narrow, padded table and pushed her face down on top of it. Her wrists were released from her back and attached to rings in the top.

There had been similar tables at the pony barn and every day, after her runs, Chocolate had been given a thorough and comforting rubdown. It was the only time her hands were freed, albeit momentarily, in order that the groom have full access to her back.

The slave girl used her strong, expert hands to ease the stress on Chocolate's back, shoulder and thigh muscles. She took her time, feeling out each one, rubbing in a strong liniment that burned as it sank into the strained flesh. But the strong but gentle hands were welcoming to Chocolate and the stinging of the ointment was quickly followed by a soothing of her muscles' aches. The young girl flipped the pony over, making sure at all times that at least one wrist was always attached to the rings at the top. She then rubbed the front of the pony's thick, hard thighs and the front of her shoulders.

To Chocolate's surprise, when the girl had finished attending to her rubdown, she leaned over her and took one of her plump breasts in her mouth.

The pull of the girl's lips on her teat caused a surge of passion to flow through the supine ponygirl. The tongue played with her stiff nipple and the mouth pulled gently on it, bringing a tingle to her loins. A strong, smooth, knowledgeable hand had seized her other breast and was kneading carefully, expertly, teasing the hardened tip, pulling on it gently.

When the girl's lips shifted to her other breast, she took her hands and slid them slowly down Chocolate's sleek sides. Chocolate could feel the hard tips of the girl's naked, voluptuous breasts on her belly, felt the softness of them mash against her. And then the lips eased their way down her torso, stopping briefly to lick the inside of her belly button, the hands moving down over her hips and caressing the outside of her thighs.

The former whore had considerable experience with female to female sex even before she became a ponygirl. Since then, she had, occasionally, experienced Sapphic delight for the entertainment of the masters. But the advances of the blond haired girl was totally unexpected, following so closely on her tortuous experience at the track and considering the beating she had suffered earlier. She felt the top of the table being lowered so that she lay fully horizontal and then her thighs lifted up and pushed back. Hot lips seized her bud of pleasure and she moaned her pleasure into her gag.

It took a while for the exhausted ponygirl to reach her crescendo of passion. But the blond headed girl was patient and used her tongue expertly between the engorged folds of her nether lips. The ponygirl's thighs rested on the blond girl's shoulders and when the girl felt them begin to quiver and shake with her impending crisis, she accelerated her loving attention to her quim. The tongue flicked back and forth over the hard button of pleasure, delved the length of her wet slit, wriggled inside her and pushed against the special spot that brought the pony ecstasy. Chocolate groaned as the first, hard contraction sent a wave of pleasure through her. She clasped her thighs tightly around the head that drove her onwards and onwards as her convulsive orgasm drove through her. Her hands strained at her bindings above her, her hips pushed hard against the mouth that enflamed her. "Ohhhhhhhh!" she moaned through her mouth filling gag. "Ohhhhhhhh! Ohhhh-hhhhhh!"

Chocolate's brown body was as limp as a rag as her cunt's contractions subsided into a mere echo of her orgasm. Docilely, she let the slave girl roll her over and reattach her wrists, one above the other, to the broad, thick leather strap that hung from the back of her collar. Weak kneed, she followed the girl's direction when she brought her to her feet and led her by the ring in her collar to a thick pallet that lay in the grass next to the pony trailer. She was thankful when the slave girl let her lay down on it and was asleep before the girl had finished locking her ankles together and strapping a thick belt around her thighs.

That afternoon, after being fed and after Giorgi had his way with her again, Chocolate was back out on the track. By now Giorgi had learned about the double duty that the ponygirl had to do. At first he was pissed, but a fatter paycheck and some consideration at maybe being able to pull one over on his brother by secretly training Chocolate to run the 3000 meter, had its appeal. All ponygirl drivers have their tricks and Giorgi was prepared to use some of his. While Chocolate watched, he mounted a heavy steel plate on the undercarriage of the sulky cart. It weighed at least thirty pounds and would add significantly to the pony's burden as she ran. He also had a pair of specially weighted boots for the ponygirl to wear. They would add two pounds to each of her footsteps. Although the practice rounds were closely watched by the touts and the other punters, only the most perspicacious would notice that the cart ran a little deeper into the soft dirt of the track or that the pony seemed to strain harder as she raised her feet.

Chocolate certainly noticed it. Her afternoon runs were agony. Giorgi was careful not to run her too hard. The extra weight ran a risk of straining her muscles. But he knew what he was doing and eased up on her, essentially letting her dog it for the afternoon.

To the brown skinned ponygirl, it seemed anything but like dogging it. After the first few laps, her thighs began to ache with the burden of their extra weight, her shoulders burned and her back screamed out in pain. There was another rubdown after the afternoon practice and the slave girl once more brought the exhausted ponygirl to sexual completion before letting her lay down on her pallet and rest.

After dinner, which Chocolate ate from a large ceramic bowl placed on the ground in front of her, Giorgi had the slave girl take the pony for a walk. Quietly, almost unobtrusively, she led the pony on a lazy stroll through the ponygirl park as if to keep the pony's tired muscles loose. It was just about dark and Ilona was able to slip out of the park and head over to the main part of the estate without notice. Waiting for Chocolate at the practice track, the track she had been training on until now, was the cruel and determined ponygirl driver. He was sitting on the sulky cart that Chocolate had trained on. The pony balked, at first, at the prospect of more running for the demonic driver, but a couple of sharp cracks of the whip brought about her quietus. She was harnessed quickly, and guided by lamps that had been set around the track, Chocolate began her training as a long distance runner.

Over the next two weeks, Chocolate became stronger and stronger. She would run in the morning without the weights and in the afternoon with them. She did not do her long distance work every night, but rather every other. A nightly disappearance might be noticed. Although the ponygirl park was for drivers, their former human charges and their slave girls only, too often friends and friends of friends came to visit. It was easier to keep busybodies away from the practice track and, after the kidnapping of Klara, Jake's slave girl, assisted by one of Burnham's Russian guards, everyone had been carefully vetted and so Giorgi and Burnham were fairly certain that there would be no leaks. The broken body of the dead traitor had been hung outside the bunkhouse for several days. The message had been clear.

Chocolate did her best to inure herself to her fate. After all, each day in training was another day closer to the ultimate race and freedom. After a few days, she got used to the incessant ordeal, her mind focused on the ultimate prize: freedom.

There was only one night when the harshness of her fate overwhelmed her. It was after all the practice for the day had been done. She had been rubbed down and then brought to orgasm both by the gifted hands of the slave girl and the fat cock of her driver. She was kneeling in the grass, her legs spread, a chain leading from her nose ring to a stake in the ground. Her body, if not her mind, was content. The night was cool and cloudless and the sky was a canopy of shimmering stars, the moon a small sliver just above the horizon. The cool breeze was refreshing and her bare nipples stiffened. The blond haired slave girl knelt next to her, gagged and with her hands bound behind her. Two naked females, one a bound and abject slave girl, but still a woman. The other one not.

Giorgi was out visiting another camp about two encampments over. The drivers were a hard drinking lot and their laughter and shouting as they teased and tormented a slave girl or two could be heard clearly.

Then one of the drivers brought out a guitar and started playing and the night was filled with the husky voices of the drivers as they sang a few of the popular Russian songs that everyone knew. They were drinking songs mostly, but then, a lone, pure male voice rose up above the rest. All the other voices became still as the singer crooned what was clearly a forlorn love song, his voice clear and soft, yet loud enough so that each sorrowful inflection could be heard.

Chocolate did not know the words, of course. Ilona, who was Latvian, and who had studied Russian in school, apparently did. She started humming softly to the tune behind her gag, a delicate counterpoint to the fine male voice. Chocolate looked over at the girl in wonder. She had hardly thought of the slave girl as more than an agent of her tormentor in chief, but when she heard the soft murmurs of her voice, she realized that she too was an innocent victim, stolen from her home, from loved ones, a prisoner to a horrid fate. Suddenly, the whole injustice of her treatment came home to her. Yes, Jake had told her it would be hard. Yes, she had agreed willingly to submit herself to it. But no one could imagine what it was really like to be treated in all respects like an animal for months and months. No one could have made her believe how tormented she would be by losing all attributes of her humanity, to be beaten again and again, to be everyone's fuck toy, day in and day out.

And then she saw the formation of a little tear escape from the eye of the slave girl next to her. It glistened in the slight moonlight and rolled down her cheek, followed by another and then another. Ilona was no longer humming, but was crying quite steadily. Chocolate began to cry too. She tried not to, but the sadness of the girl combined with her own melancholia overcame her.

When the slave girl heard Chocolate's involuntary sniffle, she looked over at her. Chocolate peered into her red rimmed eyes and a moment of humanity passed between the two females. It was only a moment. The song had ended and the group of men had resumed one of their drunken, boisterous tunes. Ilona broke eye contact with the unhappy ponygirl, pointed her face forwards and resumed her vigil for the return of their master.

When Giorgi came home, he was slightly drunk. He unbound Ilona's hands and ordered her gruffly to bed the pony down for the night. After Chocolate was bound atop her pallet on the grass outside the camper, the slave girl scurried inside. The lights dimmed in the camper and soon Chocolate could hear the muted cries of the poor blond girl as Giorgi visited some form of abuse on her body. It lasted a few minutes and, shortly thereafter, her cries of pain turned into moans of pleasure. The bound ponygirl could hear her driver's grunts through the thin walls of the camper as he gave the pretty, blond slave girl the benefit of his thick, rigid cock. There was a crescendo of passionate exclamations and then, silence. The dim interior light was flipped off and the camp was plunged into darkness. After a few moments, Chocolate drifted off into sleep.

* * * * * * * * * * * * * * * * *

The estate was a busy place as the opening day of the fall ponygirl racing season became imminent. Preparations were being made in the mansion for the huge opening day banquet. Burnham was determined to make it one to remember, had brought in extra slave girls for the event, a large swing orchestra, a hundred pounds of caviar and a supply ship load of other delicacies. Today he was busy inspecting the renovations and improvements to the grand stand which were just about complete. A long row of betting booths had been set up, a refreshment stand, luxurious boxes for the high rollers and dignitaries and a quite well appointed owners' box. There was a long string of flagpoles which on opening day would have pennants from his and the opposing team fluttering from their masts. Two large flag poles sat atop the rear of the grandstand already containing a large Kalikastani flag, which had three wide stripes on it, red, blue and gold, with a large, black, mailed fist in the center. The second flag was a large field of red on which was emblazoned the angry, black head of a mastiff, Burnham's symbol, in the center.

Burnham was meeting with the project manager in the construction office in the basement of the building. He was, as usual, pissed.

"This work was supposed to be done a week ago," he snarled at the bespectacled young engineer sitting behind the small desk. The desk was littered with papers, a half filled coffee cup, a large ashtray filled with cigarette butts and several sets of rolled up plans.

"Mr. Burnham," the man responded defensively, "the padding for the chairs just arrived yesterday. They'll be in by tomorrow night. And the floors to the owners' booth and the high priced seats are being sanded and stained today."

"But will they be dry by Friday? That's the issue. Or are my guests going to have their shoes stick to the floor?"

"They'll be dry. I have some large fans I brought in. The second coat will be on in the morning and they'll be polyurethaned tomorrow afternoon."

"Today's Tuesday, you nitwit!" Burnham screamed. "It takes 48 hours for polyurethane to set. If it rains, it'll take longer."

"The flooring came in last week. The men have been at it night and day installing it," the nervous man replied. "It'll be done, Mr. Burnham, I stake my reputation on it."

"You're staking more than your reputation on it, asshole!" Burnham sneered.

The youthful engineer quailed behind his desk. He was an American, brought in especially by Burnham to do the job. He worked for Burnham's construction company and had worked on several of his projects around the world. This had been his biggest so far. He had hardly expected the delays in importing much of the materials needed nor the almost slovenly pace of the local workers. He took a swig of his cold coffee. He had been also, he had to admit, somewhat distracted by the peculiar local customs. Even now, a comely, red headed lass knelt in the little cage that was nestled in the corner of the small office.

Burnham looked over at the cage and then back to the engineer. "I see you've had your fun while you're here. Well, imagine your balls cut off, placed in a blender and then force fed down you throat. That's what I'll have done if this project isn't completed in time. I've got a list for you and I want everything on that list done between now and Thursday morning. Got it!"

"Y,yes, Mr. Burnham."

"I don't care if you need to work all day and all night. I don't care if you've got to do the work yourself. But get it done!"

"Y,yes, Mr. Burnham", the unhappy man responded.

Outside, up on the mezzanine, Ilya Borodin, Burnham's Russian head of security had the barrel of his 9 mm Walther between the trembling lips of the Kalikastani foreman. The man had been letting his men dog it, taking long lunches to admire the naked ponygirls working out on the track, shanghaiing the ubiquitous slave girls who were running about ferrying supplied to the kitchens, washing windows, mopping floors. A broad patch of moisture was spreading around the foreman's crotch as he tried not to choke on the hard, cold, steel tube that was inserted between his lips and pressing against the edge of his throat. Several of his frightened workmen were standing around, watching with great interest. The foreman groaned as Borodin cocked the hammer of the pistol back.

"Now, am I understood completely?" Ilya asked him in Russian. Since he didn't speak the lingo, Burnham had requested that Borodin have a word with the foreman to see if he could eliminate the seeming lassitude of the work crews.

The miserably frightened foreman carefully nodded his head. He didn't want to do anything that would cause the Walther to discharge by accident. Borodin eased the hammer back down and slowly withdrew his pistol from the man's mouth. "Good," he said amiably. "And if I see any of your men standing around doing nothing between now and Thursday morning," he continued, "I'll personally come and break first theirs and then your arms and legs."

Ilya, a broad shouldered, tall, mean looking man, dressed in a finely tailored grey suit with shiny Italian shoes and a ruffled, white dress shirt, holstered his enforcer and looked around the room. The workmen all looked away sheepishly. He spoke directly to them. "And if the work is done on time, Thursday night will be a big party, with plenty of cunt to go around. Okay?"

The men all laughed and shouted their pleasure at this news.

Burnham had left the engineer's office and was about to exit the building when he looked back and saw his bodyguard and fixer, Jake sitting in the field level seats peering at the racetrack through a pair of binoculars. Burnham looked out at the track and saw the brown skinned Chocolate being driven around the far turn. He was worried about Jake. When the time came, when the Maddy business was finished, he wondered if Jake would give him a problem. Mary Ellen, the tall, beautiful gangster lesbian who was running the Elizabeth, New Jersey slaving operation took orders only from Jake. She had resisted Burnham's overtures to expand the business to the West Coast and places west of the Mississippi. That would include additional way stations, contact with criminal gangs out there and coordination with a number of different mob bosses. It was something that Burnham was going to take care of this very afternoon. But how would Jake react?

Borodin caught up with the American billionaire. Burnham looked at him expectantly. Borodin smiled. "No problem," he said.

"Good," Burnham replied. He nodded off in Jake's direction, some hundred yards or so away. "I want you to keep a close eye on him. I need him for now, but not as much as before. I value his loyalty and don't want anything to happen to him. But I want to know who he talks to, who sees him. If push ever came to shove, he's just as expendable as anybody else."

Borodin nodded. He already had his eyes on the slender, hard nosed American. He wouldn't mind putting a hole in him.

The two men descended the staircase that led down from the grandstand to the main gate. A groom was standing there and he had in his hands the reins of Burnham's work team, Flora and Dora. They were large, well muscled ponies who were past their racing years. Burnham had picked them up second hand after the spring tournament and he used them for getting around the estate. While their muscles were hard and well formed, their pale skin gave them a sheen of softness and their ample, pillowy breasts were admirable to watch as they cantered to and fro on behalf of their owner. When Burnham wasn't using them, they were often used to haul materials around the estate, or for the amusement of guests, who would take them out along the quiet country lanes surrounding the estate for leisurely runs. One of Jake's men, Tucker, had taken a shine to the big boned ponies. He was no slouch himself, over 6'4", at least 245 lbs. His features were chiseled as if from granite and he was a man of few words. Yet he cared for the almost identical blond haired ponies with affection, making sure that they were properly rubbed down and fucked every day. He could often be seen driving the pair around the estate running little errands, perched happily on the driver's seat.

Burnham and his chief henchman stepped up onto the cart and the groom handed Burnham the reins. He snapped them lightly, these were well trained ponies, after all, and the two pale skinned creatures jumped into life as if one. Their heavy boots clip clopped over the macadam pathway and their long, well groomed ponytails bounced back and forth behind them.

The mansion was almost a half mile away from the track and it took a few minutes for the ponies to deliver their passengers to the front door. Burnham and Boradin stepped off and a groom took charge of the heavily breathing ponies. The trip from the grandstand was uphill and the weight of two large men was more than the ponies were used to pulling. But they recovered quickly and the groom led them back to their barn.

The conference room was on the third floor. It was actually a converted bedroom. The prior owner of the estate, a gangster who had run afoul of the Commission which loosely governed the country, was not a corporate type and had no use for conference rooms. But Burnham had been transferring the nerve center of his world wide empire to the estate and used the room often. There was a large plasma screen monitor on the wall for conferences over the Internet, but only one telephone with a speaker in the middle of the long, dark oak table.

Telephones were kept very secure in the country since no one wanted too much news about what went on inside it to get out. The idiosyncrasies of Kalikastan were well known to various security establishments around the world, but not the precise details. It was a place often useful to the clandestine services; you could get anything you wanted there. A special CIA prison had been built about 25 miles south of the capital with its own airfield and the American government was very grateful to have it. Ironically, much of the tools of the trade of international terrorism flowed through the country as well, but when you really thought about it, from the point of view of the anti-terrorist professionals, that was ok; if the terrorists all went away, what need would the governments of the West have for them?

There were five men seated around the table when Burnham and his security chief entered. All of the men had little folders in front of them. Two of the men were Americans, men with olive colored skin and dark, black hair. They were heavy set, but not corpulent. Both had close set eyes and thin lips, as if their faces had grown inwards upon itself as a result of a lifetime of secret conspiracies. They had on shiny, dark suits with colored satin shirts and broad, flowered ties.

Opposite the men sat three men of Asian extraction. Two were Chinese. One of them wore a dark green military style tunic with bright red epaulettes on the shoulders. He was a large man with a astoundingly large stomach and heavy jowls that hung from his cheeks like saddlebags. His hair was short and had receded on the sides, leaving a peninsula of jet black hair that reached to his forehead. The other man was slight and thin. He wore black rimmed eyeglasses and a simple khaki shirt buttoned to the top. On his chest was a golden pin with a bright red star in the middle.

The third Asian man was of medium build. He wore a finely tailored suit with thin, sharp lapels. His tie was narrow and had three colored stripes cut diagonally across it. He had a large diamond ring on his right hand and a golden bracelet. His mouth was small and his features hard. His eyes were bright blue denoting his Eurasian descent. He was the only one who smiled when Burnham and his apparatchik entered the room.

"Sorry for the delay, gentlemen," Burnham volunteered as he sat in the broad, black leather chair at the head of the table. "I had some details to attend to."

There were porcelain coffee cups in front of all of the men, cream colored with gold leaf around the rims. A large plate of pastries sat in the middle of the table, although only the two Italian Americans had availed themselves of its delights. Their small, gold ringed plates exhibited the detritus of their snacks.

Burnham had had the room done over with dark mahogany paneling. A large picture window sat behind where Burnham sat giving an expansive view of the estate grounds and its appurtenances. The only decoration on the walls, aside from the large plasma monitor, was a four foot long wooden, polished shield on which was carved the black head of the angry mastiff that was Burnham's adopted heraldic symbol. The room was lit by an elaborate crystal chandelier. A single, naked slave girl stood in the corner, an auburn haired beauty, with dark eyes, plump breasts and pale skin. Her reddish hair descended to her shoulders freely. She stood next to a small table containing a pitcher of water and a large coffee carafe. Burnham signaled for her to go, and she scurried from the room happily. She had no idea what was going on between the men, but it seemed important and, no doubt, infernal. The less a slave girl knew about the businesses of the country that served as her home and her prison, the better.

"I assume that you have all read the final draft of our agreements and are prepared to proceed with our business here," Burnham stated.

The large Chinese general spoke first. His English was halting, but clear.

"All of our concerns have been properly dealt with," he intoned. "The agreement will afford us with a profitable outlet for our human and other exports and secure a safe depository for our profits." The thin man next to him nodded slightly. General Ho was the military commander of Hungzow Province, one of the most western provinces of the large Chinese People's Democratic Republic. His word there was law and the 'services' he was able to provide to the leadership in Peking was such that there was little risk of interference from the central government. His partner, Secretary Wu, was the head of the Party in the province and served as the intermediary between the general and those members of the Central Committee who were powerful enough to keep the eyes of the reformers from taking too close a look at General Ho's activities.

The slender Eurasian, Peter Wong, represented a consortium of Southeast Asian organizations. He simple smiled and said, "No problem."

The mob guys were somewhat nervous. They were used to dealing with fellow Italians and the rarified atmosphere of international dealings was discomforting. The taller, older of the two sat back in his chair. "How do we know that everybody'll hold up their end? I mean, you've got a swell set up here and all that. But can we trust you? What'll we do if you guys take our money and then whack us when we come to get it back?"

Burnham was prepared for the Americans' reservations. "Listen, markets are everything," he replied. "You have access to the largest market in the world for heroin. You also have the edge on supplying all kinds of technical products that are banned for export, something that my Chinese friends desperately want. And you have access, and will have control of when we're finished, a vast pool of delectable, young American women, something Mr. Wong's people are very interested in. I have the assurances and blessing of the National Commission to serve as the banker for your transactions and to provide, let us say, an investment house for your earnings, far out of the reach of your government. And this is just the beginning. Both Mr. Wu and Mr. Wong have assured me that they can supply you with hordes of pretty, compliant, little Asian girls to fill up your whorehouses and strip clubs. My people can send you boatloads of Russian and Ukrainian sluts that you can deal to Mexico and South America, or keep for your own uses. Then there's the knock offs. Calvin Klein, Rolex, Armani, any dvd or cd you can name. And that's just to start. The only way the system will work is if everybody makes money and feels safe. Believe me, once we get started, no one will want to fuck it up."

Giancari Franco took a deep breath. "And what are the Feds going to do while all this is going on? Sit back and watch?"

"Actually, that's exactly what they'll do. Mr. Wu and General Ho are the keys to this part of the deal. The American government has been seeking of ways to ensure the primacy of American goods and services in the biggest growing market in the world. Unfortunately, recent legislation has prevented American companies from promoting their products effectively. Nothing in China gets done without the spreading around of what we shall call 'good will'. It's illegal for American companies to do it and that has hurt our ability to compete. By using the financial facilities of our new enterprise, American companies will be able to channel funds to the appropriate decision makers in an entirely untraceable way. Not only in China, but all over the world. No money that comes through our system can be linked to any graft or bribe. Due to a friendly Administration in the executive branch, the importance of what we can provide is well recognized. We will be able, discretely of course, to widen our activities in the States and elsewhere free from interference."

"What do you mean, discretely?" Franco asked, incredulous.

"Well," Burnham replied, "as to the market in females, we can't be greedy, but I believe that we can safely cull about 2500 units a year. That averages out to about two hundred a month and should be enough, after taking into account what can be taken in the European and Canadian markets, to easily satisfy demand. Your heroin shipments will arrive safely, for the most part. You'll have to give up a few here and there for publicity purposes. But all in all, it'll be a free and clear market."

"Sheeeit!" Franco's companion replied.

"Yes, sheeeit," Burnham answered him. "And your other cottage industries, gambling, loan sharking, theft, they will be allowed to flourish within reasonable limits. As far as the current Administration is concerned, it is just the cost of doing business and gaining access to a multibillion dollar market. As to the girls, well, let's just say that they'll be doing their patriotic duty. Call it a new version of the Peace Corp. Piece of ass, that is." He smiled at his little joke.

"And you can prove this," Franco asked.

"Of course," Burnham replied. "Just give me one second." He played with the laptop computer on the table. After a moment the video monitor sprang to life. On the screen a grey haired man wearing a business suit and sitting at a large, modern style desk appeared. On the front of the desk was the Great Seal of the United States.

"Good morning Mr. Secretary, I'm sorry to have kept you waiting," Burnham said to the screen. "We've just about concluded our business."

"Very good, Michael," the man whom they all recognized said. "I wish to convey, on behalf of the President, our good wishes to your new enterprise and assure you that you will have the full backing of your government. There will be no written accord, of course, but you may rest assured that from this Administration's point of view, what's good for business is good for America."

"Thank you, Mr. Secretary," Burnham answered. "Any questions, gentlemen?" he asked as he looked around the room. The other men were silent. "Seeing none, Mr. Secretary, please give my regards to your boss. Goodbye."

The man on the screen nodded his salutation and the screen went blank.

"Well, fuck me," Franco said.

Burnham laughed. "Anytime you want, Mr. Franco. But let's finish our paperwork first."

Papers were passed around the table and signatures applied. "You understand that not all of our terms will be put into writing. These agreements merely confirm the banking details," Burnham told the men. "We're all gentlemen here and men of our word."

When the last copy was signed, Burnham rang a buzzer on the table and the door to the room flew open. Three pretty, naked slave girls entered with tall, crystal champagne glasses and a large magnum of Dom Perignon. Burnham popped open the bottle and went around the room filling the glasses. When finished he proposed a toast. "Gentlemen, to take a page from the movie *The Godfather*, I think that within a few years, we'll be bigger than U.S. Steel." Raising his glass he said, "To crime!" The men all laughed and poured the light, bubbly liquid down their throats.

* * * * * * * * * * * * * * * *

Back at the track, Jake had spent his afternoon calmly watching the ponies go through their paces. It was amazing, especially, to watch the nine pony landau in action. There were three rows of splendid looking females, their long hair flying behind them, stepping in precise unison, hauling a large, gold bedecked carriage behind them. The driver, perched high in the front, wore a black hat and the livery of an eighteenth century coachman. He had a long whip that he cracked at the leaders. Inside he coach was another man, dressed in a formal top hat and tails.

The landau was strictly an endurance race. It was the longest of the races at 4500 meters, three times around the track. The ponies had to be big and strong and perfectly disciplined. Jake had witnessed the initial training of Burnham's team and it had been a disorganized fiasco.

None of the ponies, except the two leaders, had ever raced together before. The trainers had screamed and yelled at the disconcerted ponies, liberally applying their whips as the team tried to learn to start together, maintain their pace, negotiate the turns. But here they were, running like a well oiled machine. It was amazing.

Jake was drinking a cup of coffee that had been brought to him by one of the slave girls who were scurrying around the grandstand carrying supplies and comestibles to the refreshment stands and the kitchen that served the first class seats. He had noticed that she wore on her belly the same snarling fox tattoo that Dana wore. He wondered if the fat, loquacious caterer who had gifted him Dana and had managed Burnham's banquet in the capital was running the show here. He got his answer as he saw the burly man walking along the aisle in front of the box in which he sat.

"Mr. Barnes," the man called out jovially as he approached. "How good to see you!"

Jake rose slightly in his chair to return the greeting, but the grizzled man waved him to keep his seat. He plopped himself down in the seat next to Jake.

"I'm at a disadvantage," Jake told the man. He was dressed in finely pressed blue jeans and a polo style shirt with the 2" high emblem of his training house and catering operation, the snarling fox, emblazoned on the left side over his heart. He smiled and gave Jake his hand.

"People just call me 'Danton'," he said merrily.

"Well," Jake continued," I never did get the chance to thank you properly for your gift."

"Oh, the American slave girl," Danton answered. "It was nothing. She has pleased you, I hope."

"Very much," Jake answered. He thought guiltily of how cruelly he had been treating her.

"She is a delightful creature," Danton commented, smiling. "But then, aren't they all."

"They may be delightful," Jake retorted, "but they're certainly not delighted."

Danton laughed and placed his hand on Jake's arm. "Oh, I don't know," he said. "Their fate is unhappy, that's true. But there is a certain quid pro quo that they get in exchange for the loss of their liberty."

"How's that?" Jake asked.

"Let me show you," Danton answered. A tall, thin, naked, blond slave girl was passing them carrying a carton of glasses. Danton called out to her. "Anya, come here!"

The slave girl halted in midstride and nervously approached the two men. She had a narrow, graceful face, plump lips and pretty blue eyes. Her breasts were round and firm on her chest, not large, but ample for her thin frame. Her name was highlighted in blue upon her chest and she wore Danton's symbol etched on her lower belly. Her long legs were accentuated by the high heeled clogs that she was wearing. Her torso had an appealing, curvaceous form and her hips were wide, creating a concave frame for her loins. Her hair was long and braided behind her head. She put her burden down and curtsied to her master prettily.

"Anya, this is my friend Jake. Lean over him and show him your pretty breasts."

The girl nodded anxiously and obeyed. She stood in front of Jake and, leaning over, placed her hands on the arms of Jake's chair. Her breasts were topped by short, fat nipples encircled by wide, pale areolas. She licked her lips in a sign of her apprehension. Her nipples were stiff and goose bumps had formed over the rough, silver dollar sized circles around her teats. The life of a slave girl was uncertain and being picked out by the master could easily presage an unhappy event.

Jake took the pleasing mammaries in his hands and squeezed them gently, rubbing his thumbs over the hardened tips.

"Have you come yet today, Anya," Danton asked her as he stroked her back gently with his large, hairy hand.

"No, Master," the girl replied.

"Would you like to come now, Anya" the man asked her, his voice pleasant and inviting."

The girl looked at Jake's eyes. Her face seemed to brighten at her master's suggestion. "Yes, Master," she answered meekly.

Danton had run his hand down over her firm, compact, rear globes. The girl seemed to relax and come alert all at the same time. The tip of her tongue stuck out of her mouth in the right corner.

"Then spread your legs and arch your back so I can stroke your delightful little pussy, Anya," Danton instructed her.

Anya made the suggested adjustment to her posture. Danton leaned forward in his seat and dropped his arm so that he could reach between her legs from behind. Anya's lips parted and she gave out a little sigh as Danton found her hairless nether lips with his hand. Jake still had possession of her breasts and he massaged them gently as he gazed into the girl's pleasing face.

Within a few moments, Jake could observe a change come over the girl. Her fear had all gone away. Her features had softened and her eyes had begun to water. Within a minute, her hips had started a slow, almost imperceptible gyration. Her breath had become shorter, her breasts firmer.

"Do you like that, Anya," Danton asked the impassioned girl. Her eyes had begun to flutter and it took a moment for her to bring herself back to a state where she could acknowledge her master's question.

"Y,yessssss, Master," she spoke softly. Her tongue slid from between her lips unconsciously and wetted them in a wide arc.

Jake watched the girl's face with awe. Where had she taken herself? Who was she before she had fallen prey to callous men who had stolen her life from her? What had it taken to transform her into a creature that could produce passion almost instantly at a master's command? Her English was slightly accented and Jake could not place her point of origin. Her long, blond braid had slipped over her right shoulder and brushed against his hand. Jake pulled at the tips of her teats, rubbing them between her fingers and the girl gave out a little moan. She had closed her eyes to savor her pleasure, but at Jake's action, she opened them and stared into his face. Her eyes conveyed her arousal hungrily. Her lips formed a naughty smile.

As her arousal became more acute, the girl's hips began to rock. A plume of redness had formed over her chest and her skin had begun to sweat. Her teeth bit her lower lip and her eyes rolled back. "Ohhhhhhhhh!" she moaned passionately. Her nostrils were flaring and her breath had become heavy. She tilted her head backwards exposing her long and graceful neck.

Jake looked over at Danton. He had a wide, toothy grin. "You see?" he asked Jake. The point had been made. Any reticence, guilt or shame that this girl had had in her prior life about her sexuality was completely extinguished. They were in the middle of a busy, well populated public space. Men and women were passing by right and left. She was naked and her body presented for the close examination of a perfect stranger. And yet her lusts were freely liberated. There was no reserve in her lustful responses to her master's manipulation of her sex, no holding back. "Yes," Jake concluded, this girl had gotten something in exchange for the loss of her will and her freedom. Was it enough to justify her enslavement? Enough so that she wouldn't exchange it in a moment for a return to her life? He doubted it. But it was something. Something that only her total subjugation to a master's desire could produce.

The girl was deep in the throes of her passion. She pressed her breasts hard into Jake's hands. Her hips rolled and jerked as Danton's hand drove her to completion. Suddenly, her body shuddered. Her arms, which were extended on each side of Jake's chair, began to shake. Her hands gripped the sides of the seat as if she was clinging to wreckage in the midst of a stormy sea. Her moan formed deep in her throat.

"Look at Jake, Anya!" Danton ordered. "Let him see your delight!"

Anya's head leveled and she opened her lustful eyes. Her face bore an aspect of extreme emotion, her mouth was open and her lips had formed a little 'o'. "Ahhhhhhhhh!" she called out as her orgasm struck her. "Ahhh! Ahhhhh! Ahhhhhh! Ahhhhhh!" she screamed, all the while peering obediently and deeply into Jake's eyes.

"Kiss him!" Danton ordered the girl excitedly. "Kiss him!"

The girl pressed her face forwards and covered Jake's willing lips with her own. Her lips were engorged with her passion and she thrust her tongue feverishly into Jake's mouth. Jake could feel the reverberations of her moans in his mouth as she spread her tongue along his, her lips jammed firmly against his lips. She gave a long, loud, almost anguished moan; her body quivered and then seemed to melt. She uttered a low 'mmmmmmmmmm' as she sucked as his lips languorously. When Jake took his hands from her breasts and pushed her back way from him gently, she smiled.

"Now Anya," Danton asked the still deeply breathing girl, "don't you think that you should thank my friend for his kind attentions to you?"

The girl's expression turned almost impish. "Yes, Master," she replied.

"Jake, I will leave you to Anya's kind attentions," Danton said, clapping him on the shoulder. "I'm sure that I will see more of you. Enjoy."

The fat man rose from his chair and, giving a little wave, strode purposely away. Jake turned his attention back to the thin, naked, desirable young, blond slave girl that remained bent over in front of him. She took her hands and spread them over his thighs. "May I please you, Master?" she said, her voice low, husky. Jake nodded and the girl ran her hands down his sturdy thighs and then back up again until she found his zipper. Looking frankly into his face, her right hand pulled it down slowly as her left encircled Jake's steel hard shaft still covered by the material of his pants,

The display of the girl's passionate orgasm had driven Jake's lust high. A wave of pleasure passed through him as he felt the girl stroke his manhood. When she had his zipper lowered, she took both hands and undid the belt to his pants. With practiced ease, she grasped his stiffened tool and pulled it free. She licked her lips lasciviously and bent her head down to her task.

Jake moaned as the girl's hot lips encircled him. He felt her tongue glide over the underside of his cock's bulbous head. He placed his hands on Anya's soft, round shoulders and let the delicious sensations waft through him.

The pretty slave girl took her time in pleasuring Jake's iron rod. She was kneeling between his legs and she moaned as she serviced him. Jake had closed his eyes when she had first engulfed him, but he opened them now and took in the vast racing track down below, the figures of the naked ponygirls pulling their burdens along the soft dirt pathway. A crew of workmen passed giving him knowing, smiling nods. Naked slave girls dashed back and forth in front of him.

As his lusts built, Jake's feverish mind tried to cope with the unreality of what was happening. The girl's mouth and lips were bringing him an exquisitely pleasurable experience. She was engaged in what was considered in literally the entire world as something almost shamefully private. But here he was, in a nation where the mores of the rest of civilization had been turned upside down, enjoying the girl's oral favors at this public place was as natural as walking in the park or taking in a ball game. How would he ever return to the world, he thought as the girl's tongue ran roughly down the length of his tool. How could he ever give this up?

Jake felt the tell tale surge in his loins denoting the immanency of his orgasm. He groaned as her felt his balls tighten and the tingle at the base of his cock. He arched his back as his cock began to pulse and throb in the girl's active mouth. He took his hands from her shoulders and gripped the arms of his chair. As his cock exploded, his eyes rolled back and he began to thrust mightily at the mouth that continued to enflame him. "Ahhhhrgh! Ahrrrgh!" he called out as his pleasure overwhelmed him. He could feel the flow of his spunk as it jetted out. The girl's pretty, blond head began to bob up and down as she pressed her lips tightly along his shaft and her tongue teased his cock's helmet. "Arrrrgh! Arggggh!" he called out again as the pleasure of his ejaculations exploded in his brain.

CHAPTER FIVE
THE SEASON BEGINS

It was the night before the opening day of the racing season and Burnham's party was in full swing. The celebrations had begun in the late afternoon with a traditional promenade of the ponies, all dressed up in their racing finery, before the crowd of guests at the racing track. 18 teams of ponies, each wearing either the black and gold of Burnham's stable or the red and yellow of the visiting estate pranced by the owners' box in carefully practiced steps. Chocolate had been amazed at the number of people who had come out to see them and demonstrated a little skittishness at being exhibited before such a large crowd. A rough pull on her reins gained her attention and she did her best to block it out.

The party soon moved back to the mansion and the ponygirls were all mounted at poles around Burnham's vast garden for the inspection of the guests. The garden was darkened for the occasion except for bright spotlights that focused on each individual naked ponygirl. The light was blinding, but Chocolate was still able to see the shadowed forms of the smartly dressed men and the lavishly dressed ladies on their arms. Everyone wanted a closer look at the brown skinned ponygirl which had sparked a buzz with the followers of the sport. Chocolate's ankles were spread wide, locked onto rings on either side of her and the back of her collar was affixed to the pole behind her. Several times, giggling party girls came up to feel her shaven slit and pinch her large, stiffened nipples. The rudeness and callousness of the free females surprised Chocolate. She took it as final proof, as if she needed any, that her conversion to a less than human beast was complete. She squirmed and twisted at her bonds when she felt their soft, delicate hands on her loins, smelt the delicious aroma of their fancy perfumes.

Once the band began to play, the crowd milling around the garden thinned out as people came inside to enjoy the festivities. Burnham had all the slave girls outfitted with black and gold silk caps just like the ponygirl drivers wore and short, black and gold skirts. Normally barefoot, they wore high black boots like the ponygirls wore.

Jake wandered around the party, drinking gin and sampling the delicacies from the generous buffet. Some of Burnham's popularity had apparently rubbed off on him and the elegantly clad women seemed to fawn over him. He had just taken a glass of gin from a pretty, little bare breasted slave girl when he saw someone that he knew. Before he had an opportunity to slip away into the crowd, the man espied him and he knew that it was too late. The black haired, olive skinned man strode over to him purposely. He had a slave girl in tow, with a leash leading to a ring on the outside of her gag. Her hands were bound behind her.

"Jake!" the man said loudly, shouting to be heard over the loud music from the band. "What the fuck are you doing here?"

"Hello, Mr. Franco," Jake said in reply. What he was doing here was his own business.

Burnham had invited his new business partners to stay for opening day and Franco had run through five different slave girls during that period. His sidekick, likewise.

"You hooked up with this guy, Burnham?" Franco asked.

Jake saw no way to deny it. "Yeah," he replied. "I'm helping him out." Jake had done some work for Franco back in the States. It was a messy job, but it had ended successfully.

Franco grinned broadly. "Gettin any pussy?" he asked, his even, white teeth bared.

"My share," Jake shouted back over the music. He wondered to himself what Franco was doing here. Obviously he had business with Burnham. Whatever it was, he decided that he didn't want to know.

"Well," Jake shouted back again, wanting to terminate the interview, "have a good time!"

Franco raised his right hand, the one containing the leash that led to the unhappy looking young girl behind him. "Don't worry, I am!" he yelled back.

Jake took this as an opportunity to slide away from the mobster. He pushed himself politely through the small crowd to put a safe distance between him and Franco. To Jake, this was just another sign that Burnham was getting out of hand. The mission to save Maddy had become clearly secondary to him. As if he needed it, another reminder of Burnham's madness came across his path. It was Libby, Burnham's former secretary from New York. She had been brought over about six weeks ago because Burnham felt that she knew too much about his prior illicit, but not yet outrageous, financial activities to be left behind. It had turned out, when Burnham's men searched her apartment, that she had maintained a little dossier about Burnham's long list of bribes, subterfuges and financial finagling for the purposes of blackmailing him at some yet undetermined date. She had received her comeuppance in spades. Not merely satisfied with enslaving the attractive, voluptuous, forty year old brunette, he had arranged for her body to be permanently marked in a degrading, exotic fashion.

Libby, as she was now known, when a free woman she had gone by the refined and dignified name of Elizabeth, had been completely shaved from head to toe, with the exception of the full, wiry thatch of brown pubic hair between her thighs. From the waist up, she had been tattooed in bright blue, yellow, green and red designs resembling feathers, covering her arms, face, bald head and torso, with the exception of the standard, angry, black dog that was Burnham's mark on her belly and two inch high blue florid lettering over her breasts which set forth her slave name. Her nose had been ringed. A chain ran through the ring in her slave collar connecting her braceleted wrists and forcing her hands up several inches to a spot just below her plump, multicolored breasts. This forced her elbows out, giving them the appearance of little wings. She looked like some overgrown dodo bird, and her pale, white legs and the thick patch of curly brown hair over her sex completed her animalistic appearance. It was odd, but the contrast of her mature hair and her long, unblemished rear and legs to the decorated upper parts of her body made her appear even more naked than usual.

A small crowd of guests had gathered around her, admiring Burnham's artistic use of her body. She was carrying a small tray in her loosely bound hands with little blue, green and yellow candy eggs on it. It was if she were presenting the product of her own birdlike body to them. Curious hands rubbed over her strange head and breasts while the owners laughed and made witty comments to their friends. Jake had known Libby back in the day and when she looked up at him, her eyes expressing her forlorn humiliation, a wave of sympathy passed through him for her. More collateral damage. But he did have to admit that her exotic appearance was erotically compelling. It was a rush to watch while this comely, large breasted bird woman knelt between your legs and suckled at your throbbing cock. Libby always expressed her gratitude to him for his comparably gentle treatment of her and whispered desperate, little pleas after he fucked her that somehow he save her from her fate. "Please, please, Jake, take me with you when you go. I know you can help me, please," she would say. Jake, unwilling to dash her hopes of redemption would utter noncommittal replies. She was frequently used by the guards and other male staff and few of them made any concessions to her underlying humanity. When not being used, she sat docilely, gagged and demure, outside Burnham's office at a little desk, buzzing his visitors in and out.

Shaking off his momentary feeling of sympathy for the bird woman, Jake made his way to the banquet table. He was downing a small plate of large, tender prawns when Burnham made an appearance.

The bulky billionaire had stepped up to the singer's microphone. "Attention everybody," he yelled out in his deep, commanding voice. "May I have your attention?"

Burnham was dressed in a jet black tuxedo with a large black bow tie and a white silk shirt. His pants were sharply creased. He had in his right hand a long, thin glass of white wine and in his other a chain which led to the collar of another of his recent acquisitions. It was the tall, beautiful Croatian girl that had been gifted to him by the President of the National Commission, Oscar Kasperov, at a banquet Burnham had given at his large mansion in the capital a few weeks ago. She was a former model who had foolishly accepted Kasperov's invitation to visit his homeland after a few days of partying in Zagreb. She had been ignorant of the treatment of foreign females in Kalikastan and had been shocked when she had been exposed to the sight of the pretty, naked slave girls serving at Burnham's banquet. She had also not realized that she would become a sort of 'party favor' herself until it was too late. When she was brought back to Burnham's estate, she had been relegated to the training rooms below the mansion and Jake had not seen her since then.

Burnham had allowed the tall, lithe model to maintain her long, shiny mane of black hair. She was adorned with the standard tattoo on her flat, tight belly and her name "Katya" was stenciled over her delightful, pale breasts. What Burnham had done to her formerly unblemished, sleek body was shocking. As a tribute to the female's long, slinky and curvaceous frame, he had had her tattooed with the representation of a large, colorful snake. The tail of the snake emanated from between her hairless love lips, its unseen tail presumably buried deep in her womb. Its gold, brown and red body curled itself down around her well formed thighs and up over her hip and across her belly and then back around her and up her back. It emerged over her right shoulder and curved under her breasts. Its head, long and sinister, jaws apart, venom dripping from its long fangs, was set just above the girl's pretty breasts and under her name. The rest of the comely women's skin had been shaded lightly with light brown scales that covered her arms, legs, breasts and face. Her eyes had been highlighted with indelible dark lines, giving them a sultry, evil mien and her mouth had been decorated similarly, with lines that down turned at the corners, giving her a permanent sneer. Her eyelids and mouth were painted a luxurious light green tinged with just a hint of blue, almost a turquoise. Her long fingernails were similarly adorned and she wore tall, high heeled snakeskin shoes that gave her frame a towering aspect.

It was a remarkable achievement for the artist. Burnham pulled her forward, unfastened her leash from her golden collar and, inviting the crowd to part, motioned for the beautiful, exotically bedecked woman to exhibit herself for the crowd's delight. A murmur of appreciative expressions of delight ran through the assembly of suitably impressed men and women as Katya slinked gracefully and expertly through the crowd. Jake could detect in her eyes, which darted back and forth through the excited guests, a note of the girl's terror and humiliation at this public unveiling of the debasement of her flesh. But was it really debasement, Jake thought to himself. Although the beautiful, young woman's flesh had been permanently marred, she had become a creature of dramatically alluring countenance. She was like nothing he had ever seen. As she moved through the crowd in her obviously well practiced model's prance, her hips swayed side to side, her legs crossed in front of each other, her breasts swayed and danced, tremoring with each step, bringing the brilliantly rendered reptile on her skin to life. It shimmered and curled and seemed to move all about her. It was though the creature was readying to leap off of her flesh, to seek out the observer who had foolishly presumed to cast his or her eyes on its form. The eyes of the snake were rimmed by yellow and red and were centered with the same light green that covered Katya's eyes, mouth and nails. At the end of the room, the tattooed model turned sharply on her heels, paused to let the crowd examine her at rest, and then strode slowly, but deliberately back to her beaming owner. The beast undulated on her back and her tight rear globes as she walked. Jake imagined having the strangely designed woman underneath him as he plowed the source of the multicolored reptile that twisted and turned over her body, kissing the cruel, brilliant lips, feeling the snakewoman writhe and twist underneath him. When he looked around, he could see that he was not the only one.

When Katya remounted the small stage where Burnham awaited her, she fell to her knees before him. She bent over, curving her colorfully decorated back, her long, black hair falling like a curtain around her face, and laid her lips on his shoes. A round of excited applause resounded throughout the room. Burnham raised his hands to silence them. "Quiet please, quiet," he spoke into the microphone. "I would like to introduce the genius responsible for this artistry. May I present Kendai Hyoto, master tattooist!"

A slender, short, Japanese man dressed awkwardly in his oversized tuxedo stepped self consciously onto the stage. He had very short black hair and wore golden rimmed wire framed glasses. He bowed politely to the crowd accepting their adulatory applause gracefully.

"Mr. Hyoto has agreed, in a special collaboration with Burnham Enterprises, to accept commissions from the public for his work. Later, you will be invited to view appropriate subjects that Mr. Hyoto has personally selected from our newly arrived stock for your purchase. Mr. Hyoto has provided a series of his unique designs from which you may choose, in exchange for a not inconsiderable premium." Burnham smiled at this and there was appropriate laughter from the crowd. "In the meantime," he continued, "the floor show is about to begin and so I invite you into the ballroom. Katya will be displayed appropriately for your pleasure for the rest of the evening and there will be a raffle later so that some lucky guest may sample her well developed, sexual talents."

The crowd of delighted guests wandered their way slowly into the large, high ceilinged ball room. Jake followed amidst the throng wondering what spectacular Burnham had in store. There was a large array of comfortable chairs aligned with a view of a four foot high temporary stage. Jake had been reserved a seat in the front row next to Burnham. The billionaire's chair sat in the middle of the row and was larger, almost throne like when compared to the rest. The bird woman, Libby, came in and knelt in front of him. He rubbed her bald, multicolored head absent mindedly and signaled for the house lights to dim.

In the feint light, Jake could see male servants wheeling various props onto the stage. When they fled, the sound of a low, throbbing drum beat arose, gaining in volume until its beat became heavy and almost melodic. A spotlight burst onto the stage and, signaled by the incorporation of the sound of tempestuous flutes and horns, a line of beautiful, naked, young slave girls came running onto the stage. They were all as black as coal and their skin glimmered with a brilliant sheen as if they had been oiled. They wore tufts of beige fur around their ankles and wrists and wore a headdress designed like a fury mane, descending down over the back of their necks.

The limber, agile girls made a running circle around the stage on their bare feet and then assembled themselves randomly on it, beginning a fierce, undulating, graceful dance. Their breasts, uniformly large and well formed, weaved and shook as their bodies contorted to the beat. The whites of their eyes and teeth flashed out from the blackness of their bodies. They licked their plump lips lasciviously and ground their hips invitingly to the music.

All eyes were affixed to the delectable display before the crowd. Jake felt his cock rise as he imagined taming one of the wild, African women. Suddenly, there was the sharp resounding of a whip and a tall, broad shouldered black man, black as the ace of spades, stepped out onto the stage. His long arms were heavily muscled as were his thick thighs. He carried himself with a regal grace as he centered himself on the stage. He wore nothing but a small silver thong that carried the massiveness of his sexual organs between his thighs. His head was shaven and the beams of the spotlights sparkled off of it.

At the sound of the whip, the girls, there were ten of them, had ceased their wild exertions and stood frozen, their bodies displayed in twisted, almost demonic aspects. After a delay of about thirty seconds, enough time to take in the splendid forms of the wild lionesses poised in various obscene and inviting postures, a second crack of the long, leather whip that the man held in his right hand caused the lionesses to jump back into action as they scurried to take up preordained positions around the stage, mounting the small stanchions that had been placed there by the servants. They crouched there on their haunches, their arms down between their outstretched knees, the palms of their hands next to their feet.

The almost naked black man bowed graciously to the crowd and swept his strong arm in presentation of the assembled glimmering, naked, delectable bodies around him in a semi-circle. The crowd erupted in appreciative applause. Having received the adulations of the audience, he stepped back and picked up two large black circles of wood and held them out in front of him and behind. He uttered a sharp, deep throated command in a strange, African tongue and the lion women, one by one, leaped off of their stools and took running jumps at the circles, one woman leaping through each wide circle, held about three feet off of the ground, simultaneously. The result was a constant stream of blurred, black female flesh dashing around the stage, a continuous line of motion. As they leaped head first through the circles, the women rolled over their heads and regained their feet only to make a wide arc around the stage and to leap through the other hoop.

After the nubile, shiny, black bodies had made several circuits around the stage, the man, smiling broadly to the audience, uttered another sharply toned verbal command to the women and they all remounted their original stanchions, their chests heaving with their exertions, their plump breasts shuddering delightfully. As the man tossed the rings aside, the girls snarled and undulated on their stools, carefully timing their movements with the exciting, passionate music. The black man stepped back from the spotlight and, at his command, two of the women leapt off of their stools and ran to the front center of the stage where the spotlight narrowed until it captured just their shapely, enticing forms. They began to dance slowly and gracefully together, the music softening into a dolorous, yet seductive sound. Their bodies intertwined lustfully as they kissed and stroked each other passionately. After a few moments, there was the sound of the whip and the two females broke apart and ran back to their stools as two more women took their place.

Each pair of human lionesses performed blatantly erotic routines before the crowd several times, each pairing having its own distinct character and inventiveness. Mouths found breasts, hand stroked between thighs, legs intertwined. The women uttered long, languorous moans and loud, lustful shrieks as the excitement of the moment overcame them.

Jake's cock was stiffened with desire at the sometimes languorous and sometimes wildly passionate activities of the women on the stage. He shifted himself uncomfortably in his seat and knew that some slave girl soon would have the benefit of his arousal. He looked over at Burnham and saw that the birdwoman, Libby, had her head buried between her master's thighs and was stroking his long, thick cock with her lips. His cock gave a little twitch as he recalled her expert ministrations to his own on previous occasions.

Another command roared from the tall, muscular black man's mouth and the two girls who had been performing rushed back to their perches. The man stepped forwards and took another bow before the audiences, which they responded to enthusiastically. He stepped back again and at his order, one of the pretty, maned, black skinned women hopped out to the middle of the stage. Facing the audience, she shook her hips wildly as the music's pace picked up its tempo. Whilst she was doing so, the other lionesses were adorning themselves with some kind of belt.

The first lioness caressed and stroked her hairless slit, mouthing her passion to the crowd. Her fingers slid easily into her cunt and spread her moisture around her button of pleasure. As if on a signal, she turned and slid to her knees at the right side of the stage as one of the other lionesses took her place. This one was adorned with a large, shiny black dildo held on by a strap that left her sex revealed. She grinned wildly at the audience while she stroked its length several times and she then slid down behind the other girl who was bent over, her legs spread invitingly. As the second girl eased the long, black faux cock into her sister, a third naked, black girl stepped into the circle of light.

The procession continued until all ten writhing and moaning women were linked in a long daisy chain of fornicating beasts. It was an amazing spectacle to see the beautiful, lionized black women thrusting in and out of each other. The black man stepped forwards and, ripping off his silver thong, took his place behind the last girl. His cock was long and thick and he grinned as he pushed it home into the inviting, dilated canal of the tenth fornicating woman-beast. The girls were scrunched up against one another, bent over, breasts to back. The black man waved to the audience as he plowed the slit of the supine girl in front of him. Excited by the lustful tableau in front of them, the audience exploded into cheering and applause. The group held its position for a few minutes and, at the command of its leader, the girl on the far right eased herself up and turned around. One by one all the girls did the same. When the girl who had possession of his cock slipped away from the man, he stood and ran to the other end. One by one, the girls recoupled and he took possession of the flowing, lush pussy in front of him. Grinning his pleasure to the audience, he waved again.

In the darkness, out of the side of his eye, Jake noted his boss, Burnham, stiffen and moan. Libby had completed her task and the man lurched and grunted in his chair. When he looked to his left, he saw the pretty, middle aged woman next to him. Her long, flowing, silken skirt was raised and she had her hand under it. The other hand held her breast which she had slid out from her bodice. Her mouth was open with passion and her eyes were glued on the scene of the long line of humping, moaning women. Jake resisted the temptation to satisfy himself, but he did take hold of the stiff, iron log in his pants and stroked it gently. When he looked up, the scene on the stage was changing again.

The pretty, buxom black women had regained their feet and were flowing in a large circle around the stage. As they passed the rear of the stage, they flung off their belts and the dildos that they held. On the second pass, they picked up from an invisible assistant, a black leather apparatus which, on the run, they began to strap on. A thick gag went into their mouths and, protruding from the other end was a heavy, black prong in the form of a male member. On the third circle, the first two women fell to the floor, one on her back, her legs spread open, the other on top of her, head to foot. They quickly pressed the stiff, rubbery appendages into each other's pussies and began to copulate. On each pass of the pulchritudinous, black females, another pair dropped off and formed a two backed beast, thrusting the phalluses emanating from their gagged mouths into their companion's womb.

As the last couple engaged, a large, steel cage covered with a black cloth was wheeled onto the stage and brought to the circle of mouth fucking lionesses. When the cloth was lifted, the spotlight revealed a shapely, tall, lithe woman inside. She was naked except for a wild, multicolored feathery mass around her throat, ankles and wrists. The man opened the cage and the prisoner emerged.

This woman was taller and thinner than the lionesses. She had a long, graceful face and short cropped, black hair. Her breasts were pert and firm, with long, stiff nipples that made the breasts seem to come to a point. When she stepped out of her confinement, the cage was wheeled away. The black man stood, proud and erect, his hardened manhood jutting out as the woman began a sultry, lascivious dance around him. She moved elegantly and each swing of her arm or thrust of her leg was attended to by the fascinated eyes of the audience. She laid her hands and then her lips on the muscled, shiny chest of the man and then circled behind him, running her hands over his hips, pressing her chest against his back.

She tormented and teased his flesh for several minutes and then knelt before him. Spreading her legs, she placed her lips on his hard, black rod and subsumed it into her eager mouth. The black man's eyes rolled back and he placed his hands gently on her head as she serviced him, her hips gyrating, her taut rear globes moving enticingly. She raised her ass high and her hand snaked between her thighs and began to manipulate the hairless, delicate folds there until she was able to thrust two of her long, narrow fingers inside.

The music had lowered and Jake could hear the moans and sighs of the fucking lionesses as they continued their mutual satisfactions. The man uttered a command to the woman who was servicing his loins and she stood and turned to the audience. She bent over with her long, lithe legs spread, her hands on her knees. The black man stepped up behind her. As he entered her, she moaned loudly, grimacing in pleasure.

Spellbound, the crowd watched as the black man fucked her on the stage. Her face contorted with pleasure as the man plowed her fecund channel. His face was clenched in feverish intensity as he enjoyed her hot, tight orifice. He placed his large, meaty hands on her hips and held her still as he thrust into her again and again with a mighty force. The drums of the music took command, beating a heavy rhythm in time with his thrusts. Suddenly, his head tilted back. He uttered a loud, impassioned grunt. His body shook and his hands tightened on the woman's hips. As he came inside her, the lustful woman grinned and moaned her own pleasure. Sweat was pouring down her face as she climaxed as well. She closed her eyes, her face thrust out at the mesmerized crowd. All around the couple were the sounds of the climaxing lionesses, their voices muffled by their gags. But their legs shook, their bodies writhed and their heads thrust feverishly into each other's cunts.

And then it was over. The music rose and the black man led the lovely, sated black woman back to her cage. The lionesses rose from the floor and circled the stage, casting off their headpieces. They formed a semi-circle behind the black man and, at his signal, bowed to the audience, their large breasts swaying below their chests, holding each other's hands. The black man bowed as well, his long, soft, wet dick resting between his thighs. The crowd stood and cheered, even Jake, who was normally wont to be reserved at such displays. As one, the lionesses moved once more around the stage and fled off of its rear. Slowly, acknowledging the cheers of the crowd, the black man eased himself backwards, bowing and sweeping his hands until he too fled.

The applause carried on for several minutes and the man came back out to drink in the acknowledgement of the success of his show. The lionesses came out one more time and each one, individually bowed and smiled at the audience before retreating off the stage. The man took one last, long bow and, with a waive of his hand, disappeared.

* * * * * * * * * * * * * * * * * *

Jake had pulled rank after the performance and gone behind the stage to get a closer look at the delectable black women who had made up the show. He was led down to the servants' quarters where there was a large bathroom. The women were busy taking showers, washing off the sweat and, to Jake's surprise, the makeup for the show. As each girl stepped out, he saw the blue letters of their names emblazoned across their chests and a tattoo of a fierce, snarling lion on their bellies. To his greater amazement, when he met the male star, he introduced himself with the cocky twang of a North American, urban black.

"Deke, Deke Brown," he said as he shook Jake's hand. "How'd ya like the act?"

"Outstanding," Jake replied stupefied. "I thought that, that is, I thought…." Jake stammered.

"That we was all Africans?" Derek said hopefully. He laughed. "Well, that's a big complement. I'm from Detroit."

"And the girls?" Jake asked, astounded.

"Oh, Shakala there and Layla, they're from Atlanta. The rest are from all over. Our star, Tawana, she's from LA."

"I would have never known," Jake replied. "How long have you been an act?"

"Well, this is our first real show," Deke replied. He was busily dressing in a sleek, silk lapelled tuxedo. The girls who had finished showering were dressing themselves in the black and gold caps and skirts that the other slave girls were wearing. Obviously, they were going to be made available for the guests. They would get a lot of business.

"We've been rehearsing in Dlitski for about three weeks. It took a while to assemble the cast, but Mr. Burnham's been working on it for me for a couple of months. I was running a strip joint in Vegas when some of his people approached me. I was on a plane the next day."

The girls were silently lining up against the wall, prepared for their master's inspection. They had put on the heavy, black ponygirl boots and stood there at attention. Deke had put on his tie, completing his transformation from African tribal leader to slick, suave, African American male.

"Are they all strippers?" Jake asked.

"No sir!" Brown replied emphatically. "We wanted fresh, unsullied girls." He looked over the line of naked, anxious black women. "I've got five college students, a waitress, two secretaries, an accountant and a teacher," he said proudly. "But," he added, smiling, "now they're just whores."

Deke looked at Jake. "You're Barnes, Burnham's main man?"

Jake nodded affirmatively as he perused the delectable, black female flesh. All of the girls were stunningly pretty. Their hair was cut short uniformly to accommodate their headdresses during the performance. Their eyes were bright and alert and their black skin smooth and soft. Close up, the variations in their pretty, unhappy faces could be seen more easily. They wore brass slave collars and the standard leather bracelets around their ankles and wrists. They were clearly nervous about the next stage of their responsibilities.

Deke addressed them. "All right you sluts," he said gruffly, "get out there and shake your pretty little asses. Be nice to the fancy white people and fuck like bunnies. If I hear any complaints, all of you will be very, very sorry." Deke turned to Jake. "You want one for the night?"

It was, in fact, exactly what Jake wanted. "I won't say no," he answered smiling.

"I can't give you our star, she's reserved for Mr. Burnham later. But take Jennina. She's the newest and I think she may be a little skittish in the big crowd. But she's well trained and will suck the chrome off your bumper, you know what I mean?"

Jake was pleased to take Jennina and, leaving the party prematurely, led her by a chain from her collar to his cottage. He had been allowing his slave girl Dana out of her cage and she was awaiting him dutifully, kneeling on the floor aside his large, soft bed when he entered the room. Her eyes widened when she saw the jet black female behind him. Jake lost no time in stripping and pushing the pretty, black female down on his bed. His cock was already at alert and the girl was accommodatingly moist and ready for him. The passionate woman was continuously in motion as he sawed his thick cock back and forth in her tight, hot pussy. She moaned when he kissed her, capturing his tongue with her lips and sucking on it until he groaned. When he came, she placed her heels on his thighs and pushed him deeply inside her as she screamed her own climax out loudly.

While Jake recovered, he let the two females caress and explore each other's flesh on his bed. The contrast between the pale white skin of his slave girl and the jet black skin of the lioness, for she truly was a passionate lioness, was pleasing and exciting. Later, when his forces had renewed, he toyed with Dana's plump, white breasts while Jennina mouthed his reerect organ. Deke was right. The girl really knew how to use her mouth and she made Jake come twice before she permitted his cock its freedom.

In the morning, Jake awoke splayed between the bodies of the two delectable females. He expended his morning lust by plowing Jennina from behind while watching her mouth Dana to climax.

After dressing for his morning run, he led the now demure black girl downstairs and into the kitchen. Curly and Martinez were having breakfast. They paused wordlessly when they saw the comely black lass who Jake had in tow.

"You can use her for the morning," Jake told them, "but she has to be back to the mansion by twelve. Okay?"

Curly and Martinez readily agreed and he heard them arguing about who would be first as he stepped out for his run. It was a daily ritual and he strode at a quick, steady pace over the eight miles of undulating, winding paths. His voyage took him past the vast ponygirl park and he noted the camp's activities as he went by. Ponygirls in black and gold and red and yellow hoods were being prepared for the day's events. Half of the ponies who raced could expect a severe beating before the day's end. Few drivers took losing well.

Chocolate was among the ponies being outfitted for the day's events. She had been awoken early and been shaved, showered and fed by Giorgi's slave girl, Ilona. She had expected her morning orgasm to be administered as usual, but the pretty slave girl halted her hand's manipulation of the pony's stiff clit just prior to completion. Several times that morning, to Chocolate's dismay, the girl teased and played with her, suckling at her large, thick nipples, mouthing her slit, but each time withdrawing before the relief of orgasm came to her. When Giorgi came out of his camper, he had the pony kneel down and bend over in the grass. He eased his thick cock into the anxiously awaiting, moist, hairless pussy and stroked himself there until he felt the pony's body begin to tense and shudder beneath him. He then withdrew and discharged his creamy load onto her buttocks.

The highly frustrated pony was taken down to the track and put through some warm up laps. Spectators had started to arrive and Chocolate began to experience the incipient thrill of racing day. The banners and flags were fluttering boldly in the strong breeze and the noon sun was warm and bright. Chocolate began to get nervous about her performance and the consequences of failure. She had yet to actually race another pony except for some practice heats that she had run some weeks before. She eyed the opposing ponies working out on the track anxiously. They looked big and strong and fearless. Everybody seemed to know exactly what to do but her. When she was driven back to Giorgi's encampment, her nervousness was relieved somewhat by a quick rubdown by Ilona, but her edginess was brought back to the fore again when the girl stroked her sheath until the she was panting with lust and then withdrew.

Rather than have the pony pacing nervously around a post while awaiting her turn in the racing meet, Giorgi's practice was to have her fastened securely, her collar chained directly to the post, her ankles spread and chained to rings pounded into the earth. Chocolate's anxiety grew when she heard the fanfare announcing the first race and the roar of the crowd as the ponies left the starting line.

The sulkies were always the last races of the day. The 1500 meter, Chocolate's race, was next to last with the 3000 meter the final race. But the brown skinned pony had no way on knowing when she would be called to her colors and listened to the noises of the track apprehensively. After a while, Ilona approached her and knelt between her outstretched legs, placing her expert lips on Chocolate's quim and delving her long tongue inside her. Chocolate's knees melted as the blond haired woman enflamed her, moaning her supplication through the cruel, steel bit that Giorgi had left in her mouth to be permitted to come. But the slave girl's lips left her just short of her crisis.

And then it was time. Chocolate felt numbed with fear as her harness was reapplied and she was fastened into the traces of her cart. The morning rounds had been done with the heavy boots and the extra surreptitious weight in the cart and as she towed it down the dirt track that led to the racing area, it felt lighter. The black and gold colored hooded yearlings, ponies new to their bits, had just raced and Chocolate passed them as she trotted nervously along the dusty path. They were wearing pretty garlands around their necks and the grooms and drivers of the camp were calling out their congratulations to their driver. Chocolate wondered if the naked, unknown, pale skinned former women pulling the cart were smiling as a result of their apparent victory. Their bits pulled their lips back tightly in fierce grimaces and so it was difficult to tell. But Chocolate knew that the fruits of failure would be woeful indeed and she knew how happy she would be to avoid it.

Having taken a few warm up turns in the morning had not prepared Chocolate for the full impact of the crowd at opening day. The grandstands were filled with people as was the large general admission area below it. People were lining the rail to get a good look at her as she entered the arena and Giorgi gave her a snap on her reins to increase her pace. Her whole body was a tingle from the frustrations caused by her lack of sexual release, the fear of failure and her discomfiture at being the strange object of so many people's rapt attention. Her nudity had not bothered her for many weeks, although she was disconcerted last night when the fancy people from the party had inspected her. It was the stark reminder of her obvious dehumanized status that brought her shame. How could so many people, a whole society, accept so willingly the larceny of her humanity for their mere sport? And a darker thought occurred to her. If she won, if she proved a valuable contender for the championship, why would they ever let her go?

A kiss of the whip on her behind snapped Chocolate out of her reverie. She knew that she had to suppress any distracting thoughts. She, like all the other ponygirls, had to concentrate on the now, the immediate, and let the devil take the rest.

The faces of the spectators draped over the rail at the edge of the track were just blurs to her as she trotted past them. She only had a small, dime sized size hole over each eye to see them with anyway. As she came around the last turn after having finished one warm up lap, her adversary, a pale, tall, blond tailed pony wearing a red and yellow racing hood entered the track. The cheers that emanated from the crowd clearly demarked her as the favorite. Giorgi pulled Chocolate back to let the other pony pass. Chocolate noted how her boots dug deeply into the track, pulling up small clods of earth as she ran past, the thickness of her well developed thighs, the broadness of her back. A pit developed in her stomach. "Can I beat her?" she wondered. "Am I faster?" she mused woefully. She prayed that she was.

In the stands, Jake sat next to Irkut, Chocolate's trainer. They had watched the first seven heats together, Irkut pointing out the niceties of the sport. Jake had declined, respectfully, Burnham's invitation to sit in the owners' booth. It was a little too high falutin for him. But he was in one of the luxury boxes, surrounded by well dressed, merry representatives of the local upper crust.

Jake wondered where all of the people came from. Burnham's estate was way out in the middle of nowhere, and yet there seemed to be about 3,000 people at the race. People must have traveled for days for the opportunity to attend. And some of the ritzier folk had come to the track in their own little ponygirl carts. They had arrived over the last week or so, parking their huge campers on the other side of the mansion, running their teams over the many tree lined lanes that surrounded the estate.

Burnham's teams were not doing so well. It was another reason not to be in the owners' box with Burnham. He was probably ranting and raving up there now, issuing threats and ukases about how he was going to fix the wagons of the trainers and drivers who had lost. Burnham's teams had lost five of the seven races they had run so far. Only the three pony troika and the yearlings had won victory wreaths. Having the benefit of Irkut's expertise, Jake could see how the other teams did not match up to the form and strength of the red and yellow team's ponies. Delays at the starting line, wide turns, missteps by individual ponies all were a drag on their competitiveness. They needed more time together, more experience, and there was no substitute for it.

The sulkies were different. They were one pony races and so teamwork did not play a part. It was far easier to impose your will on a single pony than a team of four, six or nine. In the sulky races, strength, speed and the experienced hand of the driver were by far the most prominent factors.

While Irkut rattled off the reasons why Giorgi was a far better driver than the other fellow, Jake watched Chocolate finish her warm up laps through a pair of small opera glasses. He could see her dark frame already covered with a sheen of sweat, the rippling of her muscles as she stepped nervously to the starting line. The entire scheme to save Maddy depended on Chocolate being a victorious ponygirl. If she could not win races, then she couldn't be in the fall tournament. If she could not champion in the 1500, then there was little chance that she could beat Maddy in a one on one race in the 3000, even if Grobgy could be induced to bet. Irkut was philosophical about it, as he could afford to be. He had explained how Chocolate's times had been good, occasionally very good, but that she had overall been disappointing. He thought that she needed another season to really develop. But since he was her trainer, as a matter of professional pride, he had bet on her. Jake had too and his 10,000 kronski ticket was in his pocket.

And then the ponies were off. A loud gunshot set them leaping from the starting line. The red and yellow hooded pony had the inside and she took a quick lead. The race was once around the track and every advantage was huge. As she gained a half length lead on the brown skinned pony, Jake's heart began to sink.

But Chocolate was digging and pumping into the track as fast and as hard as she could. She saw that the other pony had the lead and something just snapped in her. If anyone had bothered to check Jackie's records from her high school track days, they would have learned that she was a true gamer. Lazy in practice, disappointing in intrasquad matches, she was a thing truly to watch on race day. She had lost the Illinois State Championship by .04 of a second, but had smashed the records at the all city events. Like all true champions, there was something in her that hated to lose.

By the first turn, Chocolate had made up her ground. Even Giorgi was surprised by her effort. The other pony had come in as a heavy favorite and her driver had not expected much of a match. He was forced to drive his pony faster and faster as the devilish, brown skinned pony threatened to overcome their lead.

The crowd was stunned. Irkut, as sensitive to the nuances of ponygirl racing as anyone alive, jumped to his feet when he saw Chocolate meet the other pony's speed.

When the time went up on the tote board for the halfway mark, he grabbed Jake's arm and shouted with glee. Jake looked over at the excited trainer. His face was all red and his eyes were popped open. He was shouting furiously in Russian.

Chocolate's mind was ablaze with her need for victory. It was all coming back to her, the medals, the adulation, the sense of pride. She wanted it again as much as she wanted anything. She could feel her legs pumping, the collision of her ponygirl boots with the dirt track beneath her, her lungs screaming for more and more air, but was aware of nothing but the head of the other pony, inches ahead of hers.

As they came down the home stretch, the red and yellow pony suddenly pulled up. The incredible pace of the race was too much for her. Chocolate had ridden her right into the ground. With a moan, she collapsed on the track, her knees scraping the dirt, the reins pulling fiercely at her bit. Chocolate just glided past, easing her pace, knowing that she had won.

Streams of sweat were pouring down her skin in rivulets as she was taken through her victory lap. The fans were cheering wildly the startling victory of the rookie pony. While the final results would show that her success was due to the scratching of the other pony, everyone who had watched knew that a star had been born.

Chocolate was maneuvered into the winning circle where a crowd of people awaited her. Hands slapped her shoulders and rear in adulation. Giorgi leapt down from the seat and happily took Burnham's hand in a congratulatory shake. A bough of flowers was draped over the pony's head and the driver and owner were ushered next to the black and gold hooded pony for a memorial photograph. Chocolate was delirious over her victory. She would not be whipped. Even the incongruity of being treated like a race horse did not dampen her joy. In fact, she was almost proud of her victory. Her blood was still pumping excitedly in her veins and her heart had not stopped thumping. The adrenalin of victory was something that she had not experienced for a long time.

The naked, brown skinned pony looked up at the photographer as he took the shot. He clicked one off and then, holding the camera to the side, caught up in the excitement of the moment, called out to Chocolate's owner.

"One more, Mr. Burnham. Please just get a little closer to the pony."

Chocolate was startled to hear the English language spoken. But it was more than that. Hearing her owner's name was the first confirmation that she had received that Jake's plan was working. Until now, since no one had spoken to her since she was freighted to this strange country, she had not been sure that she had been delivered to the right estate, that some mistake had not been made. For all she had known, she was going to be fated to be a ponygirl for the rest of her life and Jake had either forgotten all about her or had suffered some mishap that he was unable to help her.

As the second snapshot was taken, relief washed through Chocolate's body like a wave. She had put aside her misgivings many weeks ago, knowing that the only way that she could meet the terrible demands of her trainer was to forget about everything but being a ponygirl. She felt like laughing, and she waved her bitted, hooded head in glee. When Burnham placed his heavy hand on her breast and squeezed it appreciatively, she mewed with happiness.

Giorgi backed her out of the winner's circle and took her out around the track to the exit that led to the ponygirl park. Chocolate trotted along obediently. As they passed through the ponygirl park to Giorgi's encampment, she could hear the shouts of congratulations from the other campsites. When they pulled into the grassy paddock outside Giorgi's camper, the eyes of the obediently kneeling, gagged, blond slave girl widened with pleasure as she espied the garland of flowers around the ponygirl's neck. At Giorgi's command, she quickly unharnessed the pony from the cart. She was about to take her to the shower to wash off the sweat and the dust of the track from her frame when Giorgi pushed her aside.

The diminutive, misshapen man signaled Chocolate down to her knees. He reached behind her head and freed the harsh, steel bit from her mouth. He unfastened the fly on his silk, black and gold racing pants and drew out his thick, heavy cock. Without the need for further instructions, the tall pony bent her back forwards and seized the soft, salty appendage between her lips.

Chocolate's loins began to burn as the dwarf's cock began to harden in her mouth. She knew that the small man's intent was to impress upon her, in spite of her victory, who drove her and who was ultimately responsible for making her a winner. Chocolate knew this and she gratefully eased her thick lips over the soft skin of Giorgi's heavy prick. The presence of the now hardened meat in her mouth brought a thrill to the young pony. She was giving her master his due and relished the opportunity. When, at Giorgi's command, the blond slave girl swung behind her and reached her soft, expert hand between her thighs, caressing her already moist and dilated nether lips, Chocolate was in heaven. She moaned deeply as the girl's fingers spread her engorged lips and entered her steaming tunnel. She sucked the cock of her master energetically, happily, as the hand drove her lusts higher and higher.

This morning, she had been denied relief. But she knew now that she had earned it and she let her passion flow through her like a river. The slave girl reached her free arm around her chest and began to tease her hardened, blood filled breasts, squeezing the stiff nipples, caressing the soft, firm globes.

When her pussy began to throb and convulse with hard, exquisite contractions, Chocolate yearned for the gift of her master's creamy, white spewm. She groaned as her orgasm overwhelmed her. She felt her driver's hard hands on her hooded face and he began to counterthrust against her motions, piercing her throat, pressing her face into his hairy loins. She felt him stiffen and her contractions of pleasure deep in her womb, which had been subsiding, began anew. The slave girl's hands worked her body furiously, encouraging her ecstasy. Giorgi groaned with his own unleashed lust as he pumped his seed into her.

CHAPTER SIX
A BLAST FROM THE PAST

The racing season was going well for Chocolate. Riding from estate to estate and back again in the pony trailer, her feet splayed wide and her nose ring tethered to its front, she had long opportunity to contemplate her fate. She had won every race so far but one. There had been a steady, drizzling rain the day before and the track was muddy and thick. The track officials had almost called off the day's events and waited until three thirty in the afternoon to begin the races, giving the sloppy track some additional opportunity to dry.

Chocolate had slipped going around the first turn, coating her legs in the muddy slime, and she never caught up. It was something that might have happened to any pony and was not really remarkable in a neophyte like Chocolate. But Giorgi had been unforgiving. When they returned to the paddock outside his camper, he had beat her unmercifully. Aside from lashing her body cruelly with a long, leather covered reed, he had taken a heavy club and belayed her upper arms brutally. He had the sobbing, dismally unhappy ponygirl kneel while he dug a long, three foot wide trench in the ground. When done, he pushed the errant pony into it, face first. It was just deep enough so that her torso lay below ground level. The ground was sloppy with mud and Chocolate's breasts, thighs and belly became coated with the goo. She held her hooded head up to prevent her face being coated with the sloppy substance.

She could see the dark brown mud inches from her face through her tiny eye holes. And then she heard the dwarf lowering the zipper to his pants. There was a pause and then she felt the warm, acrid product of his bladder pattering on the back of her head. She moaned in misery as the foul smelling liquid filled up the area around her face. Her hands squirmed behind her, locked in their leather bracelets and her body twisted and turned in humiliation and unhappiness.

It took a long time for the dwarf to empty himself on the unsuccessful ponygirl. Chocolate was relieved when the flow ceased. But she groaned again in misery as she felt the dwarf's booted foot press down on her head, forcing her face into the foul smelling muck. He held it there for several seconds, making sure that her hooded face was coated with the stench of his liquid waste.

Chocolate lay in her miserable hole for several hours. Finally, Giorgi relented and allowed the pretty, blond slave girl to pull her to her feet, shower and massage her tormented muscles. Chocolate did not enjoy the pleasure of her driver's prick that night, or the pleasure giving hands of the slave girl. She listened with yearning, lying bound on the ground outside the camper that night, as she heard the dwarf bring the blond girl to crisis after crisis.

In the morning all was well again and in the next race and the next, Chocolate did fine. The quality of her competition varied and she had a real run for her money only once or twice. By midseason, she was the buzz of the racing circuit. The crowds swelled everywhere that she was scheduled to race.

When they were back at the estate for home meets, Chocolate still did double training, being snuck away to the practice track on the other side of the estate to run long and hard. She, of course, could not question her handlers as to the purpose of this extra, grueling ordeal. But she was glad each time when she was loaded into the pony trailer signifying that she was being taken to an away match and that her tired legs would be given a relative rest.

Lightning had had trouble adjusting to the longer length of the 3000 meter and she suffered her driver's anger horribly. But Lightning was a fighter, and after each session of cruel abuse, locked into her little cage awaiting the closing of the camp, she would pledge herself to try harder the next time. It was at the fourth match of the season that it really clicked. She was racing against an experienced, olive skinned pony with a long, black ponytail. The track was hard and fast. The other pony was wearing a green and blue hood. Lightning got off to a good start and then led the other pony all the way.

Later that afternoon, for the first time in several weeks, she delighted in the coursing of her driver's thick cock in her needy, hot cleft, and was allowed to burst into an excited, heart thumping orgasm. After he spilled his seed deep into her womb, Jerzi had his skinny, black haired slave girl fuck the happy pony from behind with a large, black dildo. Lightning groaned with pleasure a she felt it pierce her anal opening. She swallowed her driver's softened prick eagerly when he presented it to her. The frenzied pony came twice as the slave girl plowed her ass, and once more again as her driver permitted her to swallow the semi-sweet product of his lust.

And so all was going according to plan. Burnham didn't have the time to attend each race meet and so he appointed Jake as his deputy. He was happy to be able to show himself to the successful, brown skinned pony in the winner's circle and he thought that he detected a smile from her distended lips the first time that she saw him. He caressed her face gently and stroked her breasts almost lovingly, tweaking her stiffened nipples. He desperately wanted to fuck the former Chicago whore turned female beast, but knew that she was off bounds until racing season was over. She was a delectable sight and his cock hardened when he thought of their many lustful hours together back in the States.

It was on a three day break from the racing schedule that Irving arrived. Irving Ostroff was Jake's can do man. He was a brilliant engineer and intuitive scientific detective. It was Irving that had given them the break they needed to track down Maddy after her kidnapping. But relations with Irving had been rocky since Maureen, a stocky, tall brunette that had been a prisoner in the underground prison when they overran the Georgia farm where Maddy had been held temporarily before she was shipped onwards on her ultimate voyage to Kalikastan. It had been a problem of what to do with Maureen. She had been kidnapped along with a prettier, more desirable friend and the kidnappers had been unable to unload her. They had kept her for their own amusement and that was why she was still there when Jake and Irving found her.

Irving was far from a hard case like Jake and he had insisted that Maureen be freed. Burnham, who was the client and therefore the boss, had nixed that idea. The last thing they needed was the headlines that would result when Maureen turned up to rejoin her family. There would be too many questions and it would be inevitable that the whole story of the Georgia kidnappers and the trail to

Kalikastan would be plastered all over the papers. This would tip off Maddy's captors that something had gone wrong and make it impossible for them to sneak into the country and free her.

And so, or at least so Jake thought, Maureen was to be put up in a private asylum, held incognito until the job was done. At the time, Jake had believed that it would be a matter of getting in and out of Kalikastan quickly. Events had turned out otherwise. It also turned out that Burnham had lied about the arrangements regarding Maureen and it seemed likely that he had had her disposed of as an inconvenience.

Since then, every time that Jake had spoken to Irving, he had bugged him about Maureen's fate. It had gotten to be more than a pain in the ass. It was with some trepidation that he had called Irving on Burnham's behalf a week ago. Burnham wanted to see if they could come up with a more efficient, lighter design for the sulky cart that Jackie/Chocolate was pulling. When the race came against Maddy, Burnham wanted every edge that he could get.

To Jake's surprise, Irving had agreed to fly into Kalikastan without any problem. He had not mentioned Maureen at all. Maybe, Jake thought, he was over her.

Burnham had made special arrangements for Irving to be flown in by helicopter from the capital which had the only jet airport in the country. Flights to and from and around Kalikastan were tightly controlled since it was in no one's interest to have nosey people flying in and out. Burnham had to get special permission from the National Commission every time that he wanted to use his helicopter to bring somebody to or from the estate.

The heliport had been constructed a few miles from the Burnham estate. It was remotely located in the interests of security. Burnham didn't want anyone flying over the grounds. Kalikastan was a very rough place and there was no sense creating an opening for raiders to swoop down on them. This way, any low flying aircraft over the airspace of the estate would be considered hostile and shot down immediately, no questions asked, by Burnham's security team.

At first, Jake had considered using Flora and Dora to drive out to the heliport. But he reconsidered when he remembered that Irving had no idea what the country was really like. He would get an education fast enough, but Jake didn't want to shock him first thing. He figured that he would try and explain it to him on the drive back.

Jake eased the large Mercedes next to the heliport pad and waited for Irving to arrive. He fully expected him to reopen the subject of Maureen and he was going over in his mind how he would convince him to drop the subject when the helicopter appeared in the distance. Jake got out of the car and watched it grow in size at it approached until it was there, large as life and settling down on the concrete pad like a giant dragonfly. It was a large Sikorsky, big enough for at least ten passengers. But Irving was the only one and, once the large machine settled to the ground, he hopped out, his suitcase in hand.

"Hiya, Irving," Jake said as he reached out to shake his associate's hand.

Irving ignored the gesture. Instead, he walked to the car, threw his bag into the back seat and turned to Jake and said, "Let's get going."

They drove silently back to the estate. When they came up to the mansion, about ten minutes later, a team of ponygirls was practicing on the large track. It was a four pony team and the ponies were pulling their brougham coach around the track at a leisurely pace, either warming up or cooling down. Irving took a long, cold look at the spectacle and then looked back at Jake. He said nothing.

And he said nothing when, on the entrance to the large hallway that served as a foyer to the mansion, three pretty, naked slave girls were kneeling by the door patiently awaiting instructions from somebody. Irving put down his bag. "I want to see the cart first before we speak to Burnham," he said. Jake had had the cart brought over that morning in anticipation of Irving's request.

"Okay," was all he replied, and he led Irving back outside and around to the side of the large pony barn. The quartet of ponygirls who had been being given a workout were done and they were being led into the pony barn by two grooms holding leashes that went to the rings in their noses. Irving stood and watched as the young, naked and hooded former women were led inside.

"It's over here," Jake said and Irving followed him wordlessly.

The engineer took about twenty minutes to look over the cart. He felt the rails and the steel frame. He examined the wheels. He had a little pad and he made notes of the measurements that he took. When he was done, he looked over to Jake and said, "Okay. Let's go see Burnham."

Libby the bird woman was sitting dutifully outside of Burnham's office when Jake and Irving mounted the large staircase. Jake expected some comment from Irving at the strange apparition. The desk behind which she sat had no front and her pale, widespread thighs and the hairy bush between them were readily visible as the two men reached the upper steps. Her nose ring was affixed to a ring embedded into the top of the desk. She was gagged, a thick leather shield covering the bottom half of her face. She looked up at Jake dolefully when he approached. It had been a while since he had spent any time with her and Jake took her look as an entreaty. He made a mental note to seek her out later.

"Please buzz Mr. Burnham and let him know that we're here," Jake told the elaborately tattooed woman. Her hands were affixed in front of her, a chain connecting her slave bracelets to a ring in her collar. She had to lean over to press the small buzzer and when she did, her ample, bare, multicolored breasts swayed invitingly.

Burnham had a monitor inside his office from which he could view all the security cameras all over the estate and could view his visitors outside his office. It might have been easier to let Libby announce them, but he insisted that she remain gagged at all times when not in use. His voice crackled over the intercom.

"Come on in Jake," he said and the door to his office buzzed. Jake stood by to let Irving enter first. He made a perfunctory introduction and the men sat down, he and Irving in two comfortable padded chairs in front of Burnham's aircraft carrier sized desk and Burnham in the big, black leather chair behind it.

"So," Burnham opened, "what do you think?"

Jake had winced when he saw Burnham's favorite new toy, Katya, the snake woman, ensconced in a little cage behind Burnham's desk. A tall, slender brunette with large, dark eyes and tea cup sized breasts knelt naked next to the desk. She bore red stripes across her tattooed belly and her pale, white thighs. She had long, black hair that reached almost to her waist. Her braceleted hands were up behind her head, presenting her small but lovely mounds to view.

Irving took a few moments to answer. His gaze locked on the two desirable women, first one then the other. He then looked back, almost guiltily to the American billionaire. "Well, there's a few things that can be done," he intoned in his most businesslike voice. Irving was a man of small stature. He wore wire rimmed glasses and had a slender frame. He was relatively young, about 30, but his boyish face made him look a lot younger. He had black, bushy eyebrows and a long, prominent nose. He was nerd all over.

"First of all, the steel frame can be replaced with a much lighter alloy," Irving said. "I'd replace the wooden poles with aluminum. The wheels are mounted all wrong. I'd tilt them in to get better traction. And they're too narrow for the soft dirt track. I'd widen them about an inch and a half. I'd like to do some trials first to get the width exactly right. The seat should be moved slightly over to the side, like they do in harness racing back in the States. It will help counter the centrifugal force when it's hauled around the turns. And I think I can design some better axels and gears for the wheels."

Burnham and Jake looked at the scientist with dumb amazement.

"And there's one more thing," Irving continued. "I've got a much better lubricant. It'll cut down friction on the gears by at least 20%."

Burnham smile broadly. "That's great!" he said enthusiastically. "It's just what I've been looking for. How much more speed can you get out of it?"

Irving put his note pad back in his shirt pocket. "Over 3000 meters, I'd say that you could cut down the time by about 4 or 5%, depending, of course, on the efficiency of the driver and the abilities of the woman who was pulling it."

Jake and Burnham looked at each other warily. No one referred to the ponies as women.

"You mean ponygirl," Burnham said. "They're not women, they're ponygirls."

"Funny," Irving said back coldly, "they looked just like women to me."

Burnham looked sternly back at the technical expert. Jake could tell that he was weighing whether to continue the argument or to overlook Irving's naïveté. It was one of the rare occasions that diplomacy won out.

"Yes, well, when can you get the new cart put together? There's only four weeks until the fall tournament."

Irving had been given the basics of the project on the telephone. He knew that he was being brought over to build a new cart and generally about the scheme to save Maddy. Jake had filled him in over a secure line before he agreed to come out there. Irving might be squeamish about the whole set up, but he could be trusted to keep everything that Jake told him highly confidential. He would not have lasted long as Jake's techie otherwise.

"I can probably have the basics together in about a week. There'll be some fine tuning. The final product should be ready about a week after that. I'll have the parts manufactured to specs and I'll assemble it here. But there's just one thing."

Burnham smiled. "Don't worry about the money. Price is no object. You just name a price that's reasonable and I'll pay it."

"Oh, you'll pay, Mr. Burnham, don't worry," Irving replied. "But that's not what I'm referring to."

Burnham looked surprised. Jake knew what was coming and he cringed inside. He wondered if Irving knew that he could disappear without a trace here in Kalikastan at a moment's notice. Some of Burnham's security men were lounging around in the hall just outside the door.

"What the fuck are you talking about," Burnham asked, his ire showing. What else could there be but money?

Irving rose himself to his diminutive full height in his chair. He met Burnham's stare unflinchingly. He spoke slowly, as if making sure that Burnham understood him. "Where's Maureen?" he asked.

There was silence in the room. Burnham's face was turning red like he was going to explode. "What do you mean, 'Where's Maureen?'" he retorted. "What's that got to do with anything?"

"It's got everything to do with everything, Mr. Burnham," Irving spat back. "When we were back in Georgia, you promised that Maureen would be taken care of. You said that she would be just held somewhere for a while and then allowed to go home. It's obvious that you've done something with her or you would have let Jake tell me what happened to her." Irving looked at Jake with hatred. "You've never lied to me before, Jake. You were a man of honor once. And look at you now. You've apparently taken to this evil world like a duck to water. Do you have any humanity left? How many slave girls did you rape and abuse today? How many girls have you had kidnapped and brought here, Jake?"

Irving looked as if he were about to blow a gasket. This outburst had been building up for a long time. The thing of it was that Irving was right. But at this point, what was Jake going to do about it anyway? He was in too far over his head. And he had developed a weakness for the free use of the bodies of acquiescent, pliant, submissive, beautiful young women. He started to formulate an answer, a doleful self-rationalization of his crimes, but Burnham interrupted him.

"You knew all about this many months ago, Ostroff! Don't give me this shit! I don't give a flying fuck for your quaint scruples. You've been hired to do a job and you'll do it or you'll be flayed alive and roasted over an open fire!"

"You can't make me do it against my will, Mr. Burnham," Irving answered quietly. He placed an ironic emphasis on the word 'mister' as if the billionaire didn't deserve the appellation of politeness. "I've given it a lot of thought. You're right. I take the blame for making this all possible. I knew what I was doing when I helped Jake break into the Elizabeth warehouse and take it over. I've been ruing that decision for months. And so, as part of my redemption, I decided that I don't care what you do to me. Unless you produce Maureen, safe and sound, I'm through helping you. You can do anything you want to me. Either produce Maureen or I'll do nothing. And if she's dead, and I don't send word back to my laboratory that I'm safe and sound, I'll blow the whistle on this whole scam. I've left a detailed account of this whole thing back in the States. If anything happens to me, it'll be released to the New York

Times, the Washington Post, the London Times and all the major news networks. How would you like CNN to do a story on Kalikastan, your slaving operations in the States, this evil mess?"

Burnham looked to Jake as if he was going to leap from his chair and strangle Irving with his bare hands. Jake decided there and then that if the corrupted billionaire was going to cause his long time associate any harm that he would have to go through him first. If there was a problem, then it was a problem of Burnham's own creation. Frankly, if the whole Maddy deal was going to come tumbling down like a decrepit edifice, then so be it. Maybe it was all for the better. In Jake's business, you had to be prepared to die at any time. And if he had to go in a hail of bullets while defending Irving, well, it was as good a way as any.

But Burnham seemed to get a hold on himself. Jake could see the wheels turning in his head. Burnham sat back in his large, black chair and placed his hands on its arms. Although his demeanor had changed to borderline placid, Jake could see the whiteness of his knuckles as he gripped the armrests.

"I'm sure that there's just been a misunderstanding," Burnham said. "I'll make a few calls. Why don't you go and take advantage of our unique entertainments for a while? I'll confirm that Maureen is okay and then we can get on with our business."

"If you'll pardon me," Irving replied calmly, "I don't think that I would enjoy engaging in your system of institutionalized rape. As far as making some calls, then fine. But I want Maureen produced for me here. I don't want any phone calls with somebody pretending to be her. I don't want any doctored pictures of her waiving happily by the side of some resort pool. I don't want any letters. I want to see her, talk to her, have her standing right in front of me or it's no deal."

A cloud passed momentarily over Burnham's face. It passed quickly. "No problem, Irving. But it might take me a few days. In the meantime, I'm sure, in light of your threats, that you will understand if I insist that you remain as our guest. You can fuck yourself silly all day long if you want, or not. That's your business."

The calculating billionaire turned to Jake. "I'm going to hold you personally responsible for this, Jake. No fuck ups, understand?"

Jake bristled at Burnham's implied threat. But discretion got the better part of him. "No problem, Mr. Burnham. No problem."

Burnham watched Jake and Irving leave his office with apparent equanimity. As soon as the door closed behind them, he slammed his large fists against the top of his desk and yelled, "Fuck!" The tall dark haired girl who had been fearfully watching the tense discussions quailed at his anger. Her dismal expectations regarding the fallout from the dispute were realized when the large, angry man ordered her to drape her self across the chair that Irving had vacated. Her posture exposed the back of her graceful, long thighs and the tight, pale rear mounds. The girl, an Albanian beauty spirited away from a late night party at a discothèque in Tirana, the capitol, had graduated from Burnham's slave training facility a few days before. She had only a smattering of English, but had learned most of the commands that she would need to fulfill her primary function as an object of lust. And she had already, for some sin that she was not sure of, suffered the bite of Burnham's lash. She had no illusions about what to expect from the cruel man now and she began to cry silently as soon as she buried her nose in the soft seat of the chair, her hands still obediently locked behind her head.

Burnham selected a stiff, three foot long riding crop. In his prior existence, before falling prey to the enticements of this strange sadists' paradise, he had been known to toss telephones against the walls, smash chairs, shatter vases and glasses and picture frames in acting out his mercurial anger. But now, with so many delicate, subservient young females to choose from, he had found other outlets. He raised the crop high over his head and lowered it forcefully across the proffered derriere. The meeting of the leather encased rod and the girl's tender flesh gave out a loud 'slap!' The girl moaned in exquisite pain. A long, red line of abused flesh evidenced the fierceness of the blow. Burnham, his eyes wild with unsuppressed rage gave her another and another merciless stroke. The naked, black haired girl could not restrain her misery at her suffering and moaned and cried loudly as the pain coursed through her. She wondered frantically what kind of horrible world she had become part of as she awaited the next blow. How long could she live as the defenseless object of these cruel men's lusts and brutality? Would she ever be free again?

The next blow struck the bitterly sobbing girl across the back of her well formed thighs. Its stinging kiss felt like a line of flame and the poor girl yelled out, "Yeoooooooooouuuuu!" Her hands clenched each other behind her head, tears flowed down her pretty face. As Burnham laid stroke after stroke across the tender, white flesh, each stroke seemingly harder than the last, she moaned and cried, "Yeeeeoooooouuuu! Ohhhhhhhhhhh! Ahhhhhhhhhhh!"

Burnham paused in his abuse of the delicate, delectable body of the bawling slave girl. Her legs had squirmed and jumped at each blow and her fine rear globes, tight and smooth, had danced up and down as the girl shifted her weight from foot to foot in agony. His cock was hardened by the lustful display. He tossed away the rod and released his manhood from his pants. He placed his heavy hands on the girl's curvaceous hips and angled her so that her small rear entrance was conveniently poised for his entrance.

The girl had been well trained, and as miserable as she felt at the thought of this cruel man possessing her, when she felt the tip of his stiff tool press against her dainty aperture, she tried to relax her muscles to receive him. She had learned this skill the hard way while in Burnham's basement and she had experienced much shame and humiliation as the men there forced this passage repeatedly. But no amount of pleading or screaming had made them relent and ultimately she had learned that she must cooperate in her own disgraceful ravishment or continue to suffer the physical torment of having the small entrance torn and abused each time someone developed the inclination to pierce it. But it still shamed her to be used as a man would use a boy. And it disconcerted her when, eventually, as the passage became easier for the men to navigate, that she began to experience unwanted pleasure from the rasping of their cocks along the delicate lips of her anus, that she would feel the ignition of lust as the thick meat of their pricks filled her bowels. Sometimes they would have another slave girl massage her empty, yawning slit with her mouth while she was buggered by one of the demanding, callous men. They would take her slowly, deliberately, waiting for her body to shudder in forced orgasm at the lips of another unfortunate, degraded female on her hole of pleasure to spill their hot seed deep inside her.

As Burnham's thick, steel hard rod pierced her most private place, the Albanian slave girl, still new to her trade, felt the delicate ring of flesh stretch and tear. She moaned in pain as the cock was thrust ruthlessly into her. She groaned as she felt it fill her bowels and press against the inner surface of her womb.

Burnham groaned in pleasure as he felt the moist heat of the pretty girl's ass surround his meat. The ring of flesh was tight around his cock and when he pulled back, he felt its firm pressure on the length of his tool. His excitement began to overwhelm him and, indifferent to the girl's pleasure, began to take long, hard strokes inside her.

The girl tried to fight off the strangely pleasurable effects of her abuse. But she could feel that her pussy had moistened and her breasts had become tight with incipient lust. She bit her lip to suppress her moans as the cock sent unquestionably delightful signals to her loins. The pain of penetration had passed and while the thin strips of flesh that had suffered the impact of Burnham's cruelly wielded crop still burned, the sensation of the hot iron pole that had pierced her rear drove away the pain and left only the heat.

As her lusts grew higher and higher, the girl decried inwardly what she had become. The whips and chains, the lips and cocks and hands had transformed her. Her body's revolt against her mind's attempt to bar the pleasure of her rape shamed her even as it enflamed her. "They have made me into a putanë, a whore," she thought miserably even as she yearned for the completion of her lusts.

Burnham felt his balls tighten and his cock tingle as his crisis approached. He grabbed the moaning girl's hips tighter and began to thrust harder and faster into her. When his needy cock began to throb and pulse with pleasure, he groaned and closed his eyes, his knees weakening, his mind clouding with the thrill of his orgasm. He could feel his hot juice sluicing into the girl's bowels. "Rrrrrrrrrrr!" he growled, his former anger converted into unbridled lust.

The girl whined as she felt her assailant reach his completion and the pounding of his cock within her begin to slow. Her cunt still burned with unsatisfied lust and she tightened her legs, squeezing the lips of her hairless slit together in need, pressing the small golden disks that hung there into her thighs. But Burnham had no thought for the girl's pleasure. His lust had reached its zenith and dissipated and that was all that counted. He pulled his softened cock from the girl's anus and wiped it clean with a moistened towellette from a box on his desk. As he returned his tool to its chamber, he noticed the frustrated squirming of the girl's smooth, graceful thighs. He laughed to himself and slapped her ass hard, leaving a bright, pink outline of his hand. The girl squealed in pain.

Leaving the unhappy, uncompleted girl where she was, Burnham got back to business. There was a crisis, but that was his middle name. There was much at stake. The American mobsters and the Asian gangsters that he had made his deal with would, no doubt, be unhappy if his operations were the subject of a special on "20/20". And the boys at the National Commission would not exactly be pleased. Irving was right to believe that he could upset the whole applecart. So something had to be done.

It took him almost two hours to reach the people who had done him the 'favor' of removing Maureen from the Georgia farmhouse. At first, they swore to high heaven that Maureen had been disposed of, as per his instructions. Burnham didn't believe them. No one threw away a perfectly serviceable female if they didn't have to and although the girl had been described to him as fat and ugly, the people that he dealt with had many connections. He only hoped that she hadn't been sold off to someone for a snuff film or some similar fate.

When advised that he wanted proof of her death, his contact promised to get back to him. Burnham alternatively threatened, and with the new deal with Franco and the Families that he represented, he now had real muscle to throw around, and, if not begged, made it clear that the production of a live Maureen would cause a substantial sum to devolve upon the bearer of such good news. Burnham would be on tenterhooks until the telephone call was returned.

* * * * * * * * * * * * * *

Maureen, in fact, was alive and, if not well, still a serviceable whore. She had been sold south of the border and ended up in a whorehouse known as "*La Papaya*", a punnish reference to the juicy fruit between a woman's legs. It was a place that catered to 'special tastes' and which received into its dungeon-like structure a continuous stream of unfortunate women who had lost their liberty and the ability to say no to the most salacious and painful demands of the patrons.

La Papaya lies in the city of Tuxtepec, located in the foothills of the southernmost range of the Sierra Madres. It is a pleasant, sleepy city well known for the gentility of its ruling class. But the darker desires of the upper crust needed to be served and the city was oft remarked for its string of refined and accommodating whorehouses located in the river district. *La Papaya* was one of those, but, unlike most of the others, catered to peculiar tastes. Girls, mostly kidnapped foreigners, most recently, primarily females from the Eastern European countries and the new republics of the former Soviet empire who had been lured abroad by promises of high paying jobs in the West, unwillingly staffed the house of cruelties. But they still received he occasional *Norte Americano tourista* who had lost her way.

It was three days after Burnham's frantic telephone call and Esmeralda Jaoquim, the still very becoming fortyish mistress of the house, and a hard, conscienceless procurer of slave girls, was sitting in her large salon on the second floor of the mansion watching Dr. Prado examine one of her prized possessions. Maureen was on all fours before the doctor and he was feeling her thighs and knees. Maureen was a popular attraction at *La Papaya*, but not primarily for her whorish skills, although she had refined her oral abilities greatly over the past seven months or so.

When she first arrived as a caged prisoner at the notorious house of delight, Esmerelda had seen right away that she was much too broad in the beam, too hefty in her shoulders and too plain, to put it nicely, to be a first class whore. But good staff was hard to acquire and she had put her to work immediately. Maureen needed little encouragement. She was happy that she was alive at all after being a prisoner for weeks in the underground prison at the Georgia farm. She had thought that she would die there. When Irving and Jake had rescued her, Irving had taken care of her and bathed and dressed her. He had promised that she would be safe, taken to another place for a little while, a kind of hospital and then released. She had been given an injection when the ambulance came to take her away and had awakened naked and caged. She was fatalistic by nature; her outward appearance had made her the focus of cruel treatment when she was growing up. And so she accepted her fate philosophically. And she didn't mind being a whore. She liked to fuck and before her kidnapping had not gotten many chances. But that was before the house madam had turned her into a pig.

Dismayed at Maureen's lack of success as a whore, few customers chose her even to beat or torment her, Esmeralda had gotten the idea from a customer who had refused to consider her use complaining that, "She looks like a pig!" Her face, round and somewhat flabby, she wasn't, at least until later, really fat, just 'big boned', did have a porcine look. Laughing at her inspiration, Esmeralda had made Maureen crawl naked around her room on all fours and utter little oinking sounds. Esmeralda decreed that henceforth Maureen would live her life on all fours, that she would be force fed until she gained at least 60 pounds and that she would wear a plastic pig's nose and ears and a curly, corkscrew tail. When properly fattened, she had been presented to a huge *Cinquo de Mayo* party as *La Taconera Cochina*, the pig whore. She had been a big hit and was now a sought after attraction at the whorehouse.

Dr. Prado finished his examination of the oversized, flabby, thighs and calves of the pig whore. She was wearing her pig like nose and rough, hairy, pink pointed ears. She was completely bald. She wore black, hard plastic mittens on her hands to approximate the shiny black hooves of a pig and a black, plastic cap over her knees.

"Well," Esmeralda asked, "what do you think?"

Prado laughed and smacked the large, tubby woman on her ass. "It's not a problem."

"You see, *Doctor*," Esmeralda continued, "we've been tying her legs up against the back of her thighs, but they're just getting too big. It really detracts from the overall effect."

"I can see that, Esmeralda," the doctor said, smiling. "But she really does look like a pig." Esmeralda began laughing as well.

"Yes, she does," she said. The pair was talking in Spanish, a language that Maureen still had only a rudimentary knowledge of. In fact, she was beyond caring what people said about her. Although she was dismally unhappy at being turned into a pig, her reaction was that of dull acceptance. Hadn't the boys called her that years ago? Somehow, after all that had happened to her, it was fitting. She lived now only for the frequent orgasms that she experienced on party nights when she would be the center of attention of groups of merry men. Before each party she was given an injection in her vocal chords which tightened them making every sound that emanated from her mouth turn into a high pitched squeal. The men, and their depraved female companions, loved to stimulate her to orgasm so that they could hear her moan and cry out in her squeaky voice. It made her sound just like a pig.

"It's simple, really," the doctor continued once he had regained his composure. "I can surgically remove everything below the knee and cap it off with a hard plastic shield. The hands can be removed just above the wrists and capped as well. The ends will be sore for quite a while, but after about a month, she can begin walking again. One of my assistants can fabricate some shiny black covers that will be padded on the inside."

"And her face?" Esmeralda inquired. "Can you fix the nose permanently?"

"Oh yes," Dr. Prado replied. "That and the ears. The bonding of the prosthesis will be, to all intents and purposes, permanent. I can even surgically reduce her voice box so that you won't have to give her any more injections."

"Then it's all settled," the madam concluded. "Come and pick her up the day after tomorrow. I have her booked for parties the next two nights. I have to say that some people will be disappointed at her disappearance for several weeks, but I'll promise them that she'll be back better and more pig like than ever!" The man and woman erupted again into laughter.

"C,can I hear her squeal?" the doctor stuttered between his laughter.

"Of course," Esmeralda answered. "She's had her shot about an hour ago. It takes about that long for it to really have an effect." Esmeralda addressed *La Taconera Cochina* in English. "Turn around, my pretty so that the *doctor* can see your face."

Maureen docilely turned her self on her pig like hands and knees so that she was looking at the doctor. "Now spread your legs like a good little pig," Esmeralda told her, her voice sweet and false. "Caress her breasts while I work her pussy, *Doctor*," she said to the man in Spanish. "She really likes it."

The doctor leaned over and took possession of the massive, soft globes that hung from Maureen's chest. As he caressed them, playing with the thick, long nipples, Esmeralda insinuated her hand between the pig woman's thighs and began to gently caress the plump, hairless lips that guarded her womb. Maureen shifted her body to accommodate the hand that was stimulating her and pressed her breasts into the hands of the thin grey haired man in front. She had no idea what the two people had been talking about. She didn't care. She knew that they were going to make her come and that was all that mattered.

It wasn't long before the hand of the madam was covered with the musky discharge of Maureen's welcoming pussy. The four legged girl could feel the tide of lust rising in her as her mistress teased her button of pleasure and the man massaged her pillowy globes. When the woman filled her hot tunnel with her fingers and began to simulate the action of a thick cock inside her, a high pitched, but soft whine escaped her throat.

"Take out her gag, *Doctor*, if you really want to hear her squeal!" Esmeralda told the medical practitioner. "And sit back and watch. It won't be long now!"

Prado leaned back and pulled the large, shiny red ball from the pig woman's mouth. It was shaped like an apple down to the tiny green stem that protruded from between her lips. "Ha, ha, ha, ha," the doctor laughed. "You think of everything!"

Maureen's body was in a state of bliss as the manipulation of her sex started her blood to boil. She was jerking and thrusting her hips backwards and forwards, meeting the action of her mistress's probing fingers. When the woman placed two slime covered fingers over her hardened, sensitized clit, she gave out a long, passionate moan. It emerged from her throat as "Weeeeeeeoooo-ooouuuuuuu!" Dr. Prado burst into appreciative laughter. "Weeeeeeooooou!" she called out again. Her orgasm was upon her. Her body shuddered and her breasts swung heavily beneath her. "Weeeeou! Weeeeeouu! Weeee-ooouuu!" she cried as the contractions of her pussy sent jolts of pleasure through her.

Both the cruel whore mistress and the doctor dissolved into raucous laughter. Maureen didn't mind. She was too busy reveling in the delights that the woman's hand had brought her. She was a pig, she knew it, and that was that.

When her squeals subsided, the doctor asked his client if he could enjoy the benefits of Maureen's pudgy mouth to relieve the hardness of his cock. Esmeralda consented with a wave of her hand. "Take your pleasure, *Doctor*. That's why she's here."

The doctor had just unzipped his pants and presented his hardness to Maureen's plump, open lips when the sound of marching feet were heard echoing on the marble floors in the hallway. They stopped just outside the door to Esmeralda's salon and the door burst open. A large, swarthy, bemedalled officer barged in. Esmerelda knew him well. It was Colonel Garcia, a frequent habitué of her temple of delights. But his entrance at the front of a quartet of rifle carrying soldiers was most unexpected.

La Papaya was not owned by Esmeralda. It was really owned by the head of a major cocaine smuggling organization. He called the tunes for Esmeralda and the place was often used to grant favors to officials whose cooperation permitted the smooth operation of the drug ring. Col. Garcia was one of those. But his appearance at the head of an armed group of men could spell real trouble. Perhaps a rival organization had outbid her boss and Garcia had come to arrest her. She doubted that she would arrive at the local jail alive. "Shot while trying to escape" would be the official version.

Esmeralda leapt to her feet at the entrance of the sharply dressed officer. She had long dreaded this moment, but she had had her fun and had determined long ago to meet her eventual, unavoidable end with dignity like the hard boiled whore that she was.

Her voice was cool and composed. "And what is this, Colonel?" she asked. "Are you here for business or pleasure?"

"Business, I am afraid, *Señora*," he answered in a strong, heavy, authoritative voice. "I'm afraid that I have some bad news for you."

A pit opened in Esmeralda's stomach. But her fear of death was well hidden. "So state your business, *Señor*," she said coolly.

Dr. Prado was beside himself. He was desperately trying to put away his stiffened manhood without catching it in his fly. He too had leaped to his feet and he was hopping around the room on one foot while he struggled with his piece. "C,Colonel," he stuttered, "this is most unusual. I mean, that is, I am in the middle of a professional visit! *Mio Dios*, I, I, I…"

The colonel issued a wry smile as he watched the esteemed physician's distress. Even Esmeralda, who felt herself doomed, could see the humor in it. She turned to the officer. "I am at your service, *mi Colonel*," she said.

Garcia smile broadly at the lovely whore mistress. "I appreciate your offer, *Señora*. Perhaps at another time I will permit you to enchant me with your charms. But I have come for the pig."

The statement was so comical that everyone in the room, with the exception of the doctor who was still trying to recover from his acute embarrassment, burst into laughter.

"M,my pig?" Esmeralda managed to blurt out. She was delighted that she would see another sun. But then the injustice of the officer's statement came home to her. "You can't take my pig!" As the words came out, everyone began to laugh again. The situation was extreme but ridiculous nonetheless. "Who wants my pig?" Esmeralda shouted at last. "She's mine!"

"I am very sorry, *Señora*, but my general has instructed me to remove the pig from your premises. It seems a very important *Norte Americano* has an interest in her."

Esmeralda's face widened in surprise. Had the fame of *La Taconera Cochina* spread so far? "Let him get his own pig!" she demanded forcefully. Even then she had to stifle a laugh.

"I'm afraid that you'll have to get another, *mi corazone*," the colonel stated officiously. "The pig comes with me!" The armed men behind him could not control themselves. This would be a story that would make the barracks resound with laughter for years. The colonel, realizing his comical aspect before his men turned to them and bellowed, "*Silencio!*" He was not a man to be laughed at to his face and the men sobered up quickly.

The officer looked down at the naked, hairless woman on all fours before him. He hadn't given much thought as to how he would actually remove the creature from the premises. It was clear that she couldn't walk. Fortunately, Maureen was customarily led about the building at the end of a leash and it was sitting on a table near the door. He ordered one of his men to take it in hand and to affix it to the pig woman's collar.

Maureen had been stupefied by the appearance of the soldiers. She had watched with limited understanding as her mistress and the officer had exchanged comments in Spanish. Their laughter had added a surreal aspect to the scene. But when the leash was attached to her collar by one of the soldiers, she realized that she was being taken away. In spite of her cruel treatment, she believed that being taken from the whorehouse could only make matters worse. She tried to cry out a protest, but her voice emerged as a high pitched squeal. "Weeeeeou! Weeeooou!" she called out in dismay as she felt the tug on her leash. Her porcine face with its plastic snout and the pointed, pink, hairy ears, turned red as she bleated out her pleas. But the tug on her leash was insistent and she waddled forwards on all fours obediently. The colonel snapped to attention, bowed politely and followed his men out the door.

Esmeralda stood there wordlessly as the door shut behind the departing officer, his men and her pig. She could hear their footsteps echoing down the hall as they towed her star performer away. She could hear the squealing protests of the pig woman grow fainter and fainter and then disappear. She looked over at the doctor. His softened prick, which he had been unable to retire, dangled loosely from his fly as he returned her gaze.

"*Doctor*, please put away your instrument," the whore mistress told him petulantly.

"Of course, *Señora*, of course," he replied as he tucked it away.

Esmeralda looked at the closed door. "Shit!" was all that she could say.

CHAPTER SEVEN
A THOUSAND WORDS

In the deep caverns of the Grobgy mansion, a pitiable, blond haired slave girl knelt in her little cage gazing out at the fearsome visage of her master and owner, Anton Drabik. Klara had once been, if not happy, at least content. The lot of a slave girl in Kalikastan, as anywhere else that that arcane and pre-modern institution existed, was subject to a wide range of vicissitudes, from the comeliest, pampered whore in a luxurious brothel that catered to only the refined and pedestrian in their tastes, to the lowest scrub girl in the bordellos which serviced the lowest levels of the demi-monde, where for a few kronskis, even the lowest, most scabrous client could satisfy his basest carnal needs.

The fickle winds that drove Klara's fate had cast her into the arms of a loving, caring master. Despite her underlying unhappiness at having been made into a sexual chattel, Jake had been Klara's whole world. She had found joy in making passionate love to him, watching his eyes roll back as she rode him, his manhood sunk deeply into her hot crevasse, reveling in the throb and pulse of his stiff meat as he jetted his spunk into her mouth. And he had brought her physical pleasure too, mouthing her fevered gash, giving her long, languorous strokes of his steely rod until she screamed with pleasure.

But all that was in the past. She had been stolen from him, brought to a new, strange mansion, beaten and tortured unmercifully until she revealed to her unknown tormentors everything that she knew about the only man who had given her a tender look or an affectionate caress since her almost forgotten days as a free woman back in Amsterdam.

She had fully expected to be killed after she had betrayed her master. She had actually wished for death. A former divinity student, she had prayed to God to send her to perdition for her crime. Her prayer had been answered, but not in the way that she wanted. Instead of the dark quietus that she sought, instead of finding an end to her earthly torment, the cruel, scar faced man who now sat quietly, morosely, in her cell had claimed her for his own. He had removed the disks that had hung from her labia that proclaimed her as Jake's property, and attached his own. And he had condemned her to life in this 10' by 15' cell, deep below the surface of the earth. Except when he or one or more of the other men came to torment and use her, or for the brief periods while another slave girl came to wash and feed her, she spent her time in utter darkness, either confined in her little steel cage, bound and gagged, or mounted in an exquisitely painful posture, with only her shame at her betrayal of her former master as company.

The only thing worse than the dismal loneliness she felt during her long, silent hours alone, was the wrenching fear that coursed through her body whenever she heard the rattle of the keyhole in the heavy, steel door that sealed her into her tiny, god forsaken world.

And, not content to own her body, her cruel master had stolen her soul. To her dismal shame, she had become addicted to the use of her body, come to yearn for the manipulation of her sex by the hands, mouths and cocks of her tormentors. Even the slave girls who washed her under the watchful eyes of a master would caress and stroke her, kiss the tips of her ravaged breasts, plunge their lips and tongue between her yearning labia, and force her to succumb to her body's lusts. Silent and efficient, their eyes carefully avoiding gazing into hers, as if her piteous fate was somehow contagious, they would stimulate her with their soft, gentle hands or their tender, pliant lips until her whole body shook, her mind reeled with passion and her cunt throbbed and pulsed with pleasure.

And so, during the long, dark hours of solitude, her thoughts would wander between a yearning for release, the only moments of joy she experienced, and the dread of the whip.

When the men came, they would haul her from her tiny prison, stretch her body out with chains and torment her brutally. Thus pain was always presage to their use of her. Sometimes ungagged, she would beg and plead for surcease, howl until her ears ached from the echo of her tortured voice in the tiny chamber.

At first, Klara, lost in a viral despondency, refused to eat. Her meals were presented to her in a steel bowl, a nutritious mush. But she had no desire to sustain her physical self and so turned away from it. Even the gnawing hunger in her belly could not motivate her the third time a bowl of the foul smelling porridge was presented to her. On that occasion, soon after the slave girl and the supervising master had left, the door to her cell had opened again. It was her master. Blinded by the sudden light, she did not see the special chair that he wheeled in before him. It was not until she had left her steel cage that she saw it, a nefarious apparatus if she ever had seen one. It had locks for her ankles and hands and a strange contraption where her head would rest.

Shivering with fear, the girl climbed obediently into the chair. Drabik locked her limbs into place and then forced her head to tilt back. A wide clamp went around her neck and under her chin, forcing her to look up at the rough stone ceiling. A strap went around her forehead and two plates were forced, vise like, against the sides of her head. She was completely immobile.

The cruel visaged man then forced a hard ring of rubber coated plastic into her mouth, spreading her lips widely. A tiny, long brown haired slave girl had entered with her master and was carrying her bowl of slop. Drabik removed a long rubber hose from a box on the side of the chair. It was topped with a wide, shiny, metal funnel.

When Klara saw the hose being presented to her widespread mouth, she struggled and shook in her chair, moaning her protests. She groaned as she felt it slide down her throat. Drabik signaled the slave girl and she stood on a step on the side of the chair and began to pour the offensive mixture that was Klara's meal into the funnel.

The process of forcing her meal into Klara's stomach was a slow one. The thick goo took its time sliding down the narrow hose. As her stomach began to fill, Klara cried and moaned despondently. It was as if the very last vestige of her will had been stolen from her. She wanted to perish. If she could have stopped herself from breathing by sheer force of will, she would have. In her dark prison, alone and abysmally unhappy, she had welcomed the vision of herself fading away, wasting into nothingness as her body was deprived of sustenance.

Being force fed meant that she had lost the only means that she knew of to terminate the suffering of her body and soul. When her belly was full and the offensive tube removed, her owner left her there. She tried to beg and plead for release, but her mouth was unable to form words. She continued to howl into the darkness when the dim overhead bulb was extinguished. Futilely, she struggled at the bonds that held her ankles and wrists. She jerked her head repeatedly, trying to shake off the straps that imprisoned it firmly. Staring upwards at blackness, her mouth grotesquely opened, she sobbed and wailed for hours in the pitch blackness, cursing her life, cursing her god, cursing her unbearable fate.

She had quieted down to an abject misery when the next two men came in to use her. One of them availed himself of her forcibly distended lips to thrust his thick cock down her throat while the other, kneeling between her widespread legs, brought her to a mind-crushing orgasm from behind.

Klara lost count of the number of times that she was strapped into the devilish chair and fed against her will. When she refused to exit her cage, she was encouraged by a long, fiercely painful cattle prod and placed in the chair forcibly. When finally, after what seemed to her like many days, the silver bowl was placed down in front of her, on her hands and knees, she gave a grateful sob and plunged her face into her slurry repast.

Sitting on his bench a few feet away from the dolefully watchful, caged slave girl, Drabik was lost in thought. He had used one of his many underworld connections to get a full investigation of Jake and Burnham. Klara had told him that the pair was constantly talking about a girl named

Maddy, that they had been looking for her and had found her. Drabik surmised that there was some prior connection between the girl Maddy and the pair. He had surmised that this Maddy had been recruited into slavery somewhere in Kalikastan, probably as a ponygirl and that they were trying to find her to free her. His sources had confirmed that Burnham's niece, Maddy, had been kidnapped back in the late spring. Putting those facts together with Burnham's unusual interest in the ponygirl Lightning, Drabik guessed that Lightning was the former Maddy Burnham.

Now he could have confirmed that easily by asking the pony itself. But that would have given the game away to the creature. If she thought that she was going to be rescued, it might put her off of her stride for the fall racing season. It was no good trying to get Lightning's records from Khalid's slave center, Lightning's import point. It was doubtful that Khalid kept any such records. Why would he? But even if he did, Khalid would be tipped off that something irregular was afoot. Knowledge was gold and Drabik meant to keep this treasure trove to himself. If it were true that Burnham and Jake were intent on liberating Grobgy's prized pony, this could bring the wrath of the National Commission down on the pair. Burnham was becoming quickly one of the most powerful men in Kalikastan and it would be useful to Drabik's ambitions to be able to blackmail him.

But it was one thing to believe that Maddy Burnham and the pony Lightning were one and the same creature, and another to prove it. He had ordered that his connection obtain a picture of the kidnapped girl. He had received it today. It was in the envelope that he held in his hand this very moment.

But did he really want to see it? Lightning was his passion. He would never say that he was in love with her. The notion seemed absurd. She was no longer a woman. But he was tied to her by an almost uncontrollable lust. He had never seen the face of the blue hooded pony. But he knew every inch of her supple, lusciously desirable body. What would seeing her face do to him? Given his passion for her flesh, would he be able to bear sharing it with all takers once he had a vision of her as a complete person? Or would his passion fade, his obsession with her as a perfectly obedient and devoted beast exploded? He could have told his connection to ink out the girl's face before he sent he picture, but that might have revealed too much to his trusted, but not always trustworthy source.

Drabik realized that by looking at the picture, he would be moving into totally uncharted territory. But there was too much value in knowing for sure if the identities matched to stop now.

Casting aside his dark musings, Drabik tore the envelope open. It was an 8x10" glossy, blown up from a smaller print. As he stared at the slightly blurred image of the vibrant young woman, he knew at once that he was lost.

Ironically, it was the same picture of Maddy that Jake had carried around with him for weeks when seeking out the kidnapped twenty year old. It had been given out to various police agencies in the initial stages of the search for Maddy. She was standing, waving, against a background of a pure, blue sky and the waters of a vast lake. She was in a small bikini, her ample breasts displayed invitingly, the cradle of her hips surrounding her enticingly covered loins. Drabik noticed at once the same thing that had given Jake the confirmation that he had found the stolen girl. There was a quarter sized mole over her right hip. It was unmistakable. It was the only blemish on Lightning's otherwise perfect body. He had kissed it lovingly many times as a prelude to seizing her naked love lips with his mouth and bringing the pony to a body shuddering orgasm.

The hardened killer and ponygirl trainer stared at the smiling, happy face of the pretty, young woman in the photograph. So this was Lightning, he thought. All at once, a sea of rage overwhelmed him. Why had he ever looked at it? He loathed the thought of his weakness for the ponygirl. And now, he was truly lost! Grobgy wanted to put her up against the dark brown pony belonging to the American. He virtually drooled at the thought of having the two fastest ponies in the country. Burnham had told Jake that the stake that he was placing up against Maddy was essentially the right to a load of loot in graft to be produced through the pipeline that he was building. But that was a lie. Grobgy wouldn't gamble Lightning against mere money. But to have two champions in his stable, ponies that looked as if they might dominate their events for years, that was something else. That made the game worth the candle.

But what if Lightning failed to win? Then she might be lost to Drabik forever. He couldn't bear the thought of that, especially now that he had seen her as a wholly complete woman, a being with a face, a person. Drabik cried out in a rage that sent a hard tremor of fear coursing through the blond haired slave girl awaiting his pleasure.

Tossing the fatal photograph aside, Drabik leapt up from his seat and rushed to the steel cage that housed the trembling slave girl. He unlocked the door, swung it open and grabbed her by her hair and dragged her out. He pulled her over to where a chain hung from the stone ceiling and unlocked her bracelets from behind her back.

Klara, frantically fearful of her master's rage, pulled away from him and ran to the corner of the room. Her mouth was still stuffed with its thick, leather gag and her cries for mercy and forbearance emerged as muted, incomprehensible moans. Enraged by the effrontery of the slave girl to resist her own torture, Drabik grabbed a long, supple leather bullwhip from the wall. He flung the business end at the miserable sobbing, naked, young woman and its tip landed on the top of her right hip.

Klara screamed at the piercing pain delivered by the leather whip and ran to the other corner of the room, futilely seeking a spot out of her cruel master's reach. Again Drabik reared the long bullwhip back and lashed out at her. This blow struck the poor girl on the front of her left thigh. A deep, red welt rose instantly from where it landed. Klara bent over in agony, screeching out her pleas to be spared. She had bent and turned to the wall in an effort to protect her vulnerable front and the next kiss of the whip landed on her rear, just above where the thigh meets the rotund flesh, inches away from her delicate, hairless slit. "Ahhhhhmmm-mmmmmm!" the slave girl cried into her gag. She turned back towards Drabik almost involuntarily, giving in to the instinct to protect the part of her body last assaulted.

Seeing that the slave girl's eyes were downcast, Drabik took the opportunity to cast the whip aside and quickly strode forwards to regain a purchase on the slave's long, blond hair. Klara went limp in abject fear as the furious killer dragged her roughly across the stone floor back to where the chain hanging from the ceiling awaited her. Fruitlessly, Klara pummeled the hand that held her hair in a tortuous grip, crying and pleading into the thick wad of leather that filled her mouth and stifled her words. Drabik grabbed her thin right wrist with his free hand and lifted her up bodily until it was with the range of the clasp on the end of the chain. He swiftly released the struggling girl's hair and fastened the clip to the ring in her slave bracelet. Klara was writhing and kicking at him, punching at his solid, muscled chest with her free hand. When he grabbed it and imprisoned it as well on the dangling chain, she moaned deeply and went limp.

Drabik stepped back from the captured female. His blood was truly up. There was none of the cool, calculated, controlled passion that he usually displayed when engaging in the pleasurable experience of making a slave girl dance to a whip. He truly wanted to bring harm to the poor, sobbing female. It was more than the fact of her resistance. That just served to push his explosive passion past the boiling point. It was the fact that this was Jake's slave girl, his lost treasure. If it were not for Jake, Burnham would probably never have found Lightning. If it were not for Jake, Burnham would not have been able to find a ponygirl to challenge Lightning to a match race. If it were not for Jake, he would never have had to view the happy, innocent face of his obsession. He could have gone on satisfying his burning desires for union with the ponygirl without conceding her humanity, without seeing her as a proper object of real, human love. He might have been able to continue to deal with her possession by other men, overlooked the fact that someday she would be no longer useful as a ponygirl and be sold on.

All of the killer's hatred focused on the defenseless flesh of the sobbing, blond haired slave girl before him. He stepped to the wall and pulled on the end of the chain that led from there to a ring in the ceiling and down to the girl's bound wrists. He lifted the girl up until her toes scraped the cold cement floor. Tying off the chain, he took two steps, retrieved the bullwhip from the floor and turned to face the symbol of his nemesis.

There was just enough room in the cell for Drabik to effectively swing the long, twisted, leather whip. Klara had jolted back into alertness when her body was lifted and she stared at the demonic man, her eyes wide in panic. Her body shivered at the rage bespoken by Drabik's angry eyes. She had no idea what had sparked his madness, it didn't really matter. But she knew from what she saw in the killer's face that this whipping would be like no other.

Drabik struck out with the long whip with all of the force that his strong right arm could bring to bear. The end of the whip curled and snapped just as it touched the top of Klara's dangling, rotund right breast. Klara's body stiffened in exquisite pain and she shouted her pain into her gag at the top of her lungs. "Ahhhhhhhhheeeeeee!" she cried out. Even the thick wad of leather in her mouth could not suppress the volume of her exclamation. A deep, maroon bruise rose immediately from where the whip had struck her and a tiny rivulet of her blood began to trickle down over her fear stiffened nipple.

Blinded by his own rage, Drabik struck out at the girl's breasts again, landing this blow on her left one, just to the right of her wide, dark areola. Klara's body convulsed with the pain and she shook her head wildly as she screamed again, "Ahhhhhhhhhheeeeeee!" Blood bubbled up from her torn skin.

The two blows did not take the edge off of Drabik's rage. The sound of her lamentations, the sight of her bruised and damaged breasts, drove him on. He lashed out at her tattooed belly, her wildly flailing thighs. He swung behind her and covered her ass and back with large, blood colored welts. After the tenth blow, he paused. His breath was coming hard from his exertions, her body was sweat soaked. His cock was hard with lust. But he was not finished punishing the physical embodiment of the absent object of his hatred. Stuffing the end of the whip in his belt, he went behind the miserable, sobbing wench and lifted her legs up, one by one behind her. He affixed each ankle to other chains that were strategically placed in the ceiling of the cell for just such a purpose. Klara's legs were spread wide, her legs curved upwards. Her posture was as if she was making some ungainly dive through the air. Knowing the new target for her master's wrath, Klara wriggled and jerked her legs insanely in a vain effort to hide away her tender, plump nether lips.

Drabik was not deterred by the girl's frantic struggles. He threw his right arm back and jerked it forwards, pulling back at just the opportune moment. The whip landed with a loud 'crack!' and the slave girl howled. The soft, pale skin of her pussy's lips erupted in a blossoming of red. Her body shook and quaked as it tried to diffuse the deadly pain. Again he struck out and again until the length of Klara's defenseless slit was an angry, swollen maroon.

Finally, Drabik was sated. As the girl continued to howl and sob, he tossed the whip to the floor. His body was limp from the expenditure of his raw emotion. A small cabinet of liquors was kept in the room for the convenience of the masters and Drabik walked slowly over to it and, pulling out a half filled bottle of Stolichnaya, brought the stem to his lips and drank two large mouthfuls. He closed his eyes and bent his head back as the fiery liquid descended down his throat. He took another hearty swig, relishing the swimming of his brain as the alcohol had its effect on him.

Glancing back at his sobbing victim, a wave of lust passed through him. He placed the bottle down on the table and walked up behind the swaying, grotesquely displayed girl.. Her reddened pussy looked back invitingly at him from between her upturned legs. He needed to make a small adjustment to the strange posture of the helpless girl and so he went back to the walls and lifted her legs up higher by the chains that connected to her ankles through the ceiling rings. Klara whined as she felt her body being moved, obviously distressed at the suggestion that her abuse was to continue. Drabik stepped in between her arched up legs. Her pussy was now tilted slightly upwards at the level of his mouth and he could have access to the little bud of pleasure at its tip.

He reached his hand out and touched the damaged flesh around the girl's love hole. It was hot from its torment and Klara gave a squeal of pain as he pressed the swollen labial lips together. The skin was turning a deep purple where the lash had kissed it. Drabik squeezed the lips hard and Klara moaned in pain. The twin golden discs denoting his ownership of the girl's flesh hung down on either side of the damaged slit. They bore Drabik's personal crest, an etching of a snarling hyena, fangs bared fiercely. The hyena, much despised, was a vicious animal, capable of anything. And that was Drabik all over. It was who he wanted to be. He would ignore the smiling face that he had seen in the picture a mere half an hour ago. Lightning wasn't a woman anymore. She had no more connection to the woman in the photograph than did the unhappy blond Dutch girl here before him. He vowed that when the comely, brown tailed ponygirl was returned to him after the fall tournament, he would whip her body raw and excise his lust for her once and for all, destroying her in the bargain if need be.

The cold hearted killer stepped forwards and placed his tongue between the brutalized lips of the blond slave girl's sex. Her body shuddered when she felt it. His hands were on the insides of her undamaged thighs, spreading them widely. He ran his tongue the length of the girl's slit, down to her bud of pleasure and drew the small point of flesh into his mouth.

The warmth of Drabik's mouth upon her cunt was a strange counterpoint to the burning ache of pain that emanated there. At first, the tingling that it sparked was faint and subsumed by the throbbing pain where she had been struck. But when the cruel man's tongue began to tickle and massage her point of pleasure, the sensation of the slave girl's unwanted lust began to overcome the still strong residue of pain.

Drabik knew his way around a cunt and soon had the girl's crevasse moist and steamy. He caressed her cool thighs gently, in spite of his rough hands. He slid his long, fat tongue along the length of the hot gash again and again until the girl moaned. He then drove it deep within her, caressing the soft, musky inner surfaces.

Klara groaned with a combination of unhappiness and pleasure as Drabik took her now hardened nub delicately between his sharp teeth and pulled on it. He licked at it with the broad part of his tongue, letting the little button drag along it. He took his hands from the panting, sobbing young woman's thighs and reached out for her bruised and damaged breasts. Flicking his tongue over her engorged clit, *rapidimento*, he tickled the nipples, tugging on them gently. He then circled the large, dangling mammaries with his hard, strong hands and squeezed them tightly. The injured flesh sent harsh signals of pain to Klara's brain, mixed with the exquisite sensations brought on by the man's active tongue.

The slave girl didn't know whether to moan in pain or cry out in pleasure. The two sensations overwhelmed her. Her lust grew and grew until her distended thighs began to shudder and her breath became heavy. She tried to close her thighs to prevent her passion from reaching its culmination, ashamed and appalled that the man who had brought her such unbearable pain could so easily bring her such intense, unwanted pleasure.

When Drabik felt the girl's thighs press against the sides of his head, he gave the drooling, fully flowered pussy three long, languorous licks with his tongue along its entire length and then reseized the girl's stiff clit with his lips and sucked at it hard. Klara gave out exclamations of her pleasure, crying out "Mmmmmm! Mmmmmmmmmm! Mmmmmmmmmmm!" as her crises began to crest. When she came, her whole body jerked and spasmed as her pussy throbbed and contracted. Her suspended body writhed as wave after of wave of pleasure flowed through her. She clamped her teeth down fiercely on the leather plug that filled her mouth giving out a long, almost mournful moan, "Mmmmmmmmmmmmm!" as her tormentor's tongue drove her on and on.

The musk of Klara's pulsing cunt fueled Drabik's lusts. He unfastened her legs from the chains that held them suspended and let them drop to the floor one by one. The slave girl's body was limp and exhausted from her ordeal and when her tormentor released her wrists she collapsed to the floor like a dynamited building. Drabik grabbed her by her hair and pulled her callously to her knees. He released her gag from her still moaning mouth and unhoused his rampant cock from his pants. He pulled Klara's head back by her hair and glared into her anguished, wet eyes. "Suck my cock, cunt, or I'll give you ten more lashes with the whip!" he snarled at her.

Klara looked up and saw the fierce determination in her owner's eyes. All of her wanted to crawl back into her cage, to curl up into a little ball and close her mind in on itself. But she knew that there was only one road to peace. Her lips trembling, her hands free for once of fetters, she opened her mouth and accepted the stiff, thick tool of her oppressor.

Her efforts at pleasing her master were, at first, dulsatory. Her enfeebled lips encircled the hard meat and her tongue washed over the bulbous head. But she could only mount a feeble effort at bringing pleasure to her master's pole. Drabik pulled her head back and slapped her fiercely twice across the face, causing the girl to screech at the shock of the hard man's open hand on her cheeks. Sobbing, her face marked deep red where she had been struck, Klara opened her mouth to beg for a surcease to her torment only to have Drabik's conscienceless tool force its way between. Her piteous pleas stifled, the fearful girl forced herself to her task. Placing her hands on her master's thighs, she pressed her swollen lips hard around the shaft and twirled her tongue around the plump helmet. Drabik forced her head down to his belly and she swallowed the salty, cruel meat.

Having compelled the slave girl's cooperation, the callous killer tightened his grip on Klara's wild, yellow mane and drove her mouth up and down his needy cock. He closed his eyes and bent his knees as the heat of her now active oral cavity sent a torrid wave of pleasure through him. He was the master. He took what he wanted. Neither Jake, nor Burnham nor his despised boss, Grobgy, would stand in his way of what he desired. The unhappy sounds of the slave girl's gurgling throat each time he delved deeply inside it was like a confirming chorus to the aria of his depraved thoughts. He groaned as he felt his fluids rising, thrusting back at the mouth madly.

The man's abuse of her mouth and throat triggered something in Klara. Somehow, all the pain and humiliation she had felt during this long, tortuous session with her master seemed right. She deserved to be punished, deserved to suffer. She deserved to be the depository of her tormentor's spunk. She had betrayed the only man who seemed to care for her. She had experienced mind wracking pleasure from the tongue and lips of the man who had stolen her soul. "Do it! Do it!" she thought as she struggled to suck on the steel-like wand that pummeled her. "Give me your spunk! Pollute me! Punish me!" she demanded silently as Drabik's sword of flesh rode over her lips and tongue again and again.

Finally, Drabik's cock began to jerk and spasm within her. Her mind exploded with a perverse pleasure as she tasted his viscous discharge filling her mouth. Drabik groaned his pleasure as he came, his deep, fearsome voice echoing through the small chamber. His hands seized the sides of her head and pressed hard into it, as if her were trying to crush her skull. When his last, throbbing ejaculation was spent, he held his cock poised deep inside her esophagus, as if to prolong as long as possible the reverberations of his orgasm.

Klara was coughing and struggling for air when he released her. She fell to the floor, limpid from her ordeal. Drabik stood over her, taking in her piteous form. Her body was covered with deep purple wounds; blood still trickled from some of them. It had smeared across her skin in places, giving her the appearance of having been painted in deep red. Satisfied at his handiwork, he knelt down and rolled her to her stomach, grabbing her arms and relocking her wrists behind her. Turning her to her back, he forced the thick leather gag back into her mouth. Reaching to her feet, he locked her ankle bracelets together. He raised her legs into the air and dragged her back to the chain which had recently held her wrists aloft. He fixed the rings of her ankle bracelets to it and then pulled the chain high so that the slave girl dangled upside down above the floor.

Klara moaned with pain and unhappiness as her body swayed helplessly. She watched as her master, her evil god, picked up a crumpled envelope from the floor. He turned and opened the door to her cell and slammed it shut behind him. The sound of the heavy, steel door crashing closed still echoed through the small room as the single, dim bulb on the ceiling was extinguished. When it died, the only sound in the pitch black, dark room was the heavy, morose peals of the slave girl's sobs.

End of Book Six.